Chocky's Challenge

Chocky speaks:
'. . . *cosmic energy. It is a source of infinite power, and so of infinite possibilities . . . I intend to explain all of this to you. Cosmic energy costs nothing. It is freely available and unlimited. It can never be used up. It will last as long as the universe itself . . .*'

'It's a dream,' whispers Wade, '*the* dream . . .'

CHOCKY'S CHALLENGE

MARK DANIEL

A Thames Magnet Book

Magnet paperback edition first published 1986
by Methuen Children's Books Ltd
11 New Fetter Lane, London EC4P 4EE
in association with Thames Television International Ltd
149 Tottenham Court Road, London W1P 9LL
Novelisation copyright © 1986 Mark Daniel
Scripts copyright © 1986 Anthony Read
Storyline copyright © 1986 Premier Video Ltd & Anthony Read
'Chocky' copyright © 1968 The Estate of John Wyndham
Printed in Great Britain

0 423 02120 6

I'm not qualified to write this.

My knowledge of astrophysics is acquired from 'Twinkle, twinkle' and my mathematical studies stopped at the twelve times table.

I explained all this to Meyer when first he approached me to do the job. I also told him that I was a sceptic. I had no experience of extra-terrestrial emanations and, to be honest, at first believed that those young and brilliant brains had been affected by the sheer scope and intensity of their work. I was wrong. I know that now.

'It doesn't matter,' Meyer told me. 'The publisher says that you write fast. We need this book published quickly. The general public has to know what these children have been through. I think that's the only way that they will be able to carry on with their work in safety. I want everyone in the kingdom to know what they are working on and who has been trying to stop them.'

So here we are.

Chapter one

With his eyes closed, Matthew can see with startling clarity. The green of the Scholars' Lawn, the gold of the towering chapel, the cinder-grey stones of the Senate House: all are vividly present.

He knows that this building is King's Chapel. He has seen it on television and on record-sleeves at Christmastime and on a picture postcard from Albertine just a couple of months ago. The postcard told him nothing. There was nothing to tell, but they nonetheless exchanged postcards from time to time. Telepathy isn't everything.

Down here in London, big, bruise-coloured clouds barge one another across the high studio window. A cold, watery breeze wriggles in under the door. But in Cambridge it is a lovely day. He grins as he closes his eyes. He can almost feel the weight of the sunlight on his shoulders. He can almost hear the tinkling and creaking of the bicycles and the rustle of crisp cotton. He can almost smell that scent of lawns which lingers on floral prints and jeans.

His eyes flick open. He sketches the Senate House with rapid, fervent strokes. Again and again the pencil rises as the sun catches a window and makes it gleam brighter than the sky. His tongue-tip sticks out at the corner of his mouth. He is picking up on Albertine's excitement as she draws near . . .

Despite the weather, Harold Meyer wears tweeds. His steel-capped shoes click on the pavement as he pushes his aged and blistered black bicycle up King's Parade. Albertine wheels a bicycle too, but she is dressed for the weather. Her bike is lime green and gleaming new. It has drop handlebars and lots of gears. She is dressed in floating white cotton all covered with tiny pink spots. Her floppy straw hat came from the Oxfam shop. She trimmed it herself with that ribbon, those pink silk flowers.

Her father's hand clasps her shoulder and squeezes. '. . . too much,' he is saying, 'I mean, you've worked incredibly hard. Really. And you've got all the ability in the world. But it takes time, you know. Simply in physical terms, it takes time. One year, you know, well . . .'

'It's all right, Daddy.' Her voice is calm. She gives him a thin little smile over her shoulder. 'Don't worry. It's all right.'

She props the bicycle against the railings. Already a small crowd stands waiting on the Senate House steps. A few eyes swivel as Albertine and her father squat to lock their bicycles. Some students down on the lawn murmur to their neighbours and nod towards her. One, a lean, blond man in a tailcoat crosshatched with grass clippings, points at her with a champagne bottle.

Albertine is trotting up the steps now. Once or twice she exchanges a greeting with another student. Her father follows. He climbs two steps at a time, his hands on his knees. He looks down at his feet.

The crowd around the notice board defers to Albertine's diminutive stature. It parts to let her through.

'Are they up yet?' Harold Meyer growls behind her.

'Hold on.' She stands on tiptoe and scans the

8

boards. 'Modern Languages ... History ... Yes! Oh. Here we are. Maths ... Um ...'

Matthew sees it even as she does. 'Oh, well done!' he whispers. He slams the pencil down. 'Well done, Albertine!'

For he knows that they are one step nearer to their goal.

'Well, now we can get on with the real work,' Albertine calls across to her father. They mount their bicycles and push off towards Peterhouse. 'We must go and see Professor Ferris this afternoon.'

Harold Meyer shakes his head and grins, approving. 'Well done, lass.' He stamps down hard on the pedal. 'We showed them all right, didn't we? Absolutely fantastic. Nothing can stand in our way now. They'll have to give us a grant for the research.'

'Yes,' she nods seriously. 'Yes, I think so ...' She glances down to her right. 'What's this idiot doing?'

Her bike wobbles. A long blue car slows at her side. The near window squeaks down. 'Hello. Miss Meyer, isn't it?' A mottled pink head emerges, encircled by wisps of sandy hair. The eyes that look up at her are pale blue and bulbous, the skin talcum dry. Fat judders beneath the eyes and at the jawbone.

'What do you want?' Meyer calls.

The baby-faced man ignores him. 'Many congratulations, Miss Meyer.' His voice is a clogged and husky whine. 'Bolus, *The Sun*. How does it feel to be the youngest ever graduate of this University?'

'Very nice, thank you,' Albertine says drily. She switches a quick grin on and off.

'What are your plans now, Miss Meyer?'

'To get on with her work uninterrupted,' Meyer

snaps over Albertine's head. 'If you want to talk to my daughter, you may make an appointment with me.'

'Miss Meyer . . .' Bolus persists regardless, but Meyer's bike swerves around Albertine's.

'You seem to forget, Mr Bolus,' he barks, 'that my daughter is only fourteen years old. She is therefore in my charge. I have repeatedly told her not to talk to strangers. You are a stranger. Kindly leave us alone to get on with our work.'

'All right, all right,' Bolus mumbles as the window closes. 'Cocky old crank. I dunno. Poor bloody bluestocking brat . . .'

The car shudders, rumbles a bit on its own account, then roars as it accelerates, swings into Silver Street and is gone.

'Matthew!' His father's voice. The bang of the front door. A quick gust of wind that shakes the window. 'Matthew! Are you set?'

Matthew shakes his head and stands. He pulls the door open and runs to the top of the stairs. 'Hi, Dad,' he grins down at David Gore. 'Yes, I've got all the pictures ready. They're in the living room, all except for the big Egyptian one. I couldn't get that down on my own.'

'OK. I'll give you a hand.' Gore climbs, one hand on each banister. 'We've got to get moving, old boy. I'm sorry I'm late, but I got held up at work. The people at the gallery will be waiting for us. We've only got – what? Six, six and half hours before the exhibition opens.'

'OK.' Matthew leads him back into the studio. 'I'm all ready.'

'Nervous?' Gore picks up one end of the plain

brown wooden frame and nods to his son. 'One, two, three, hup!'

'No, not really.' Matthew backs through the door. 'It'll be all right.'

'Not afraid of the reviews?' Gore grunts. 'London debut at fourteen. They'll be looking to put you down, you know.'

'I know, but I think it'll be fine.' The frame bumps against the banister. 'Dad?'

'Yup?'

'What's a starred first?'

'Something I wish I'd got.' David Gore grins. 'It's the best sort of degree you can get. Why? Albertine?'

'Yup.' Matthew nods proudly. 'She was top of the whole exam list.'

Gore whistles. 'Was she indeed? Well done, Albertine. It's incredible. After only one year. Incredible. Still,' he fumbles with the front door handle, 'I suppose with Chocky . . .' He stops in the doorway and frowns. 'But hang on. I didn't think the results were published till tomorrow.'

Matthew shrugs, 'They went up a few minutes ago.'

'Then how . . .?' Gore's eyes roll up towards the grey sky. 'Oh, of course, I'm still not used to the fact that you can pick up the news from Cambridge without increasing my telephone bill.' He lifts the hatchback of the station wagon. A red double-decker grumbles past. '. . . be thrilled,' he says.

'What?'

'I said, I imagine she must be thrilled.'

'Mm,' says Matthew. 'She is.'

In the early afternoon Albertine and her father set off again towards Christ's College where her Director of

Studies has his rooms. Thanks to Chocky, Matthew can see Albertine when he chooses and, of course, when she chooses to be seen. At the moment, he is too preoccupied with hanging his pictures in the Asmussen Gallery in the Halkin Arcade and she with the forthcoming interview.

She frowns and looks grim as again she parks her bike in Hobson Street. A quick fresh breeze lifts her fair hair from her brow. Without a word to her father, she leads the way round the corner, in past the Porter's Lodge and round the first court.

Albertine clatters into Tree Court and swings round into the dark doorway. She trots briskly up the bare stone staircase and knocks twice.

'Come!' a rising, reedy voice from within, like a single staccato note on the oboe.

Albertine pushes open the door. Her father puffs a little as he catches up. Albertine looks about her. For a moment, in the half-light, she can see no one. Books and linenfold panelling make the walls very dark. The only light comes from the courtyard. It pours in a streak through the leaded windows. Beneath it, the parquet is white as sun-bleached herringbones.

Something moves in the corner to her right. She turns. Professor Ferris is no more than a disembodied shock of wiry white hair, somehow suspended in the shadows.

'Ah, my dear, my dear!' He turns and approaches. He stoops a little, but is still very tall. 'Princess Zara, no less.'

'Who?'

'Princess Zara. Gilbert and Sullivan, my dear. Another young lady who attained a high degree. At Girton too. Here, my dear.' He shows her with

12

exaggerated courtesy to a high-backed leather chair. 'A little glass of sherry to celebrate.'

Albertine sits stiffly. 'You're forgetting again, Professor.'

'What?' he starts. 'Oh, yes. Stupid of me. You'd better have this, Meyer. Sit you down, sit you down. Orange juice for you, my dear?'

'Please. Lovely.'

'I do wish you'd hurry and grow up, young lady.' Ferris returns to the shadows. Something clicks. Something gurgles. 'I can't get used to having a pupil who's too young to drink sherry. Now, then, here your are, my dear. I think we might allow ourselves the luxury of a small toast. To Albertine. Many congratulations on your quite extraordinary achievement.'

Albertine smiles, a little nervously now, and shifts in the enormous chair. Her feet do not touch the ground. Meyer drinks quickly, then lays down his glass. He clears his throat. His fingers flick impatiently through the sheaf of papers on his thigh.

'Ah, yes. Now.' Ferris saunters slowly round to the desk. One long white finger stabs at the lamp. Light snaps on. Meyer blinks. 'The important question is, what next, eh? I'm afraid you won't actually be able to collect your degree for another two years.'

'We know that,' says Meyer.

'It's the regulations, you see. Age old. Have to keep nine terms before you can graduate.'

'Yes.' Meyer is almost curt. 'We know that.'

'I think it's a silly regulation.'

'Do you? Ah, yes, maybe, my dear. But then, there are reasons for these things, you know, even if you think them silly. First, it's a tradition of the university, and tradition, though far from inviolable, has something sacred about it. And there again, it prevents abuse, you see. There have been times in our history when many a rich young man or woman would have been delighted to pay a fixed sum and call himself MA Cantab. This regulation, you see, prevents that sort of thing. You have to keep your nine terms, and anyone who keeps nine terms here must, I think, have learned something by the end. And finally, most undergraduates actually need three years. We don't get many who can do it in less than one. Matter of fact, I don't think we've ever had anyone like you before. Not in eight hundred years.'

Albertine blushes and says, 'Sorry. Of course,' in a little voice. Meyer's lips twitch downwards in a quick grin of pride, then he goes back to drumming his fingers on the papers. He sighs.

'The thing is,' says Albertine, 'that I want to do some research.'

'Of course, my dear, of course.' Ferris picks up an empty pipe. It clatters on his teeth, then pops regularly as he sucks on it. 'But what sort of research?'

'Cosmic energy.'

Ferris stops popping. 'Cosmic. . . ?'

'And anti-gravity.'

'Anti-gravity?' Ferris almost squeaks. Then, 'Interesting concept, must say. Could there be such a thing?'

Albertine shrugs, 'Could there be such things as quarks?'

'Yes. Yes, quite,' Ferris muses, the pipe now back in position. 'My word, young lady, you do choose the most difficult areas. Anti-gravity indeed. Where would you begin? Anti-gravity . . .' he loses himself in the concept. His ghostly white hand extends and

14

pushes upward against the air. It casts moth's wing shadows on the wall behind him.

'I shall begin with anti-gravitational waves in space,' Albertine says softly. Ferris does not hear. His long fingers slowly clench as though to squeeze the juice from the still air. Meyer clears his throat again. Albertine leans forward. 'I shall begin with anti-gravitational waves in space.'

'Ah.' The hand drops. 'Ah, I see. You'll be moving over from pure mathematics to astrophysics then?'

'That's right, Professor,' Meyer snaps. 'Would you mind?'

'No. No. Not at all. Very interesting field, astrophysics.' He stands. 'Well, you'll have to let me have some proposals, something a little more specific, of course, before the university can consider funding you. Funds, as you know, are not plentiful. No one is exactly flush these days, and there will be others competing for the grant. You realise that, of course. We'll need something pretty special to persuade them. Think you can manage that?'

'Yes, Professor,' says Albertine, 'I think I can manage.'

'Course she can.' Meyer also stands. 'Well, Professor, we must be going. We've got to be in London by six-thirty.'

'Oh,' the white eyebrows rise. 'Bit of a celebration, hmm?'

'No,' Meyer says shortly. 'An art exhibition. Friend of Albertine's. Private view.'

'Good, good.' Ferris lays his hands on their backs and steers them towards the door. 'Very important, a bit of culture. Always afraid, with really bright pupils, that they may lose that sense of magic, that sense of mystery, which is so essential to all good science.

15

Don't want to become mere ledger-keepers, do we?'
'No,' says Albertine.
'Hmm,' says Harold Meyer.

Chapter two

The whole bright room laps and clinks and purrs. It's like a lake full of bottles.

Matthew is the hero of the hour, but it doesn't feel much like it to him. From his height, the whole world seems made up of flashy silks and pinstriped suits which jostle him this way and that. Cigar smoke battles with Estée Lauder and loses. Great open breakers of English vowels crash over him. Words like 'darling' and 'Marvellous' and 'to think!'

He puts his head down and works his way towards the rear of the gallery. He feels superfluous. Everyone seems to be marvelling that these pictures were executed by one so young, but they don't seem to connect the concept of the young artist with the reality of the boy. An astrakhan coat and a huge belt buckle suddenly shove his right shoulder. He catches a glimpse of a droopy moustache and granny glasses as he staggers sideways into a silky black and white stomach. Someone says 'Whoops!' A glass glints as it jerks upward, then cold liquid seeps down his collar and splashes on his sleeve. He says 'sorry', then wonders why.

'Matthew! Matthew! Over here!'

He grits his teeth and heads towards the source of the sound. As a mmm-ah kissing couple part, he sees his father. He barges straight into another man who gets in his way (whose exhibition is this, anyhow?) and jumps up the steps to his father's side.

'Seems to be a great success!' David Gore yells into his ear.

'Is that what it is?' Matthew laughs.

'Yup. Look at all the red tags. You've sold – what – seventy per cent already. Poor old chap. Not your sort of thing, really, is it?'

'Not really.'

'Nor mine. Have you had some food?'

'Nope.'

'Come with me. The gannets haven't got the lot.'

Gore leads him to a table. He picks up a plate and piles it high with vol-au-vents and sandwiches. 'Here,' he says, 'get yourself round that. I'll get you something to drink.'

A moment later, with cheeks puffed out like a hamster, Matthew has a glass of golden bubbly stuff shoved into his hand.

'Dad – is this . . .'

'Champagne. Yes it is. Reckon you deserve it.'

Matthew sips, grimaces and grins. 'Hey! I like that!'

'Yeah, well, don't develop too much of a taste for it . . .' Gore turns as a dark, middle-aged woman taps his shoulder. She is encased in a stern, smart, dark blue suit. A black tie splays over a perfect white shirt.

'Mr Gore?'

'Hello.'

'Pru Gibson. May I have a word with your quite brilliant son?'

'Fire away,' Gore shrugs. 'Quite Brilliant Son, this is Ms – Mrs? Mrs Gibson.'

'Congratulations, Matthew!' she gushes. 'I'm most impressed. Really.'

'Thanks you,' says Matthew.

'Most impressed. You must have done a great deal of travelling.'

'Er . . .' Matthew casts a quick, desperate glance at his father. 'Er, not exactly, no.'

'But all these views – New York, Hong Kong, Moscow – you don't mean that they're drawn from *photographs?*' She spits out the word like an obscenity.

'Oh, no.'

'They're impressions,' Gore steps in. 'They're Matthew's impressions as to how these places must be.'

'Ah. Fascinating. From what you've seen on films and television and so on?'

'Something like that,' Matthew nods. 'Yes.'

'In that case, I'm even more impressed. Quite remarkable, really quite remarkable.'

She moves away murmuring. Matthew looks up at his father. His eyes twinkle. He sighs and pretends to mop his brow.

Then suddenly he frowns. His eyes shut. His head jerks up. A happy smile tugs at the corners of his mouth. 'Good,' he says. 'Yes, come on.'

He swings round and looks down at the doorway. Gore too turns. He knows what is happening. He can guess, at least. Then Matthew is waving and jumping up and down. Meyer and Albertine stand in the doorway.

It takes Albertine just half a minute to sidestep through the throng. Matthew holds out a hand for her as she jumps up the step. She is flushed and happy.

'Albertine,' he grins.

'Matthew.' The moment's pause that Gore has come to expect, as rapid thoughts – the news, perhaps, in telepathic shorthand – passed between them, then, 'Isn't this exciting!'

'Mmm,' Matthew nods. 'Hello, Mr Meyer.'

'Hello, Matthew.' Meyer essays a smile. 'You must be jolly proud. A one-man show at your age. Well.'

'Yes.' Matthew's eyes are still locked on Albertine's. 'I am. Thanks.'

'No prouder than you two must be.' Gore approaches with brimming glasses. 'Hello, Albertine. Congratulations.'

'Thanks, Mr Gore. Of course, having Chocky around helped.'

'Even so. It's like we said to Matthew when he saved his sister Polly. You remember? When Chocky somehow taught him to swim and he pulled her out? Chocky may have taught him, Chocky may have taught you, but you both had to have the guts and the will and the stamina to learn and to do what you did.'

'She'd 've got a first in any case,' Meyer drones. He taught Albertine. He risked imprisonment in order to do so. He was prosecuted for refusing to send her to school. He always knew that his Albertine was a genius. He still cannot quite accept that she has been receiving extra-terrestrial extra tuition. It rankles. 'Just taken a bit longer is all. Two years, perhaps, 'stead of one.'

'Come on,' Albertine grasps Matthew's upper arm. 'Let's go and see these pictures.'

'I've done a new one of the windmill.'

'What's that you've got there, champagne. . . ?'

The crowd opens like a stage curtain and falls shut behind them.

'How's she coping now?' David Gore leans back against the trestle table. 'With Chocky, I mean?'

'Oh, she's coping fine. It's me that finds it all a bit difficult.'

20

'I know what you mean.' Gore gives a heartfelt grin. 'Oh boy, do I know what you mean . . .'

David Gore is referring to his experiences with Chocky – or rather, to his experiences with Matthew when Chocky first turned up.

'Well, what would you have thought?' he asked me. 'I mean, OK, we've all heard of children with imaginary companions, but suddenly here was Matthew not only talking to this invisible friend, but arguing, and arguing logically. Then it was the binary system. Suddenly, in his school maths books, we found that he was using binary. And he'd never been taught it at school. He just said that Chocky said it was more logical. My wife damned near had a breakdown. Not surprising. We thought – God knows what we thought. We just weren't equipped to think that Chocky might really exist.

'Then came the paintings. Suddenly, Matthew was painting and drawing really well – subjects he'd never seen before, yet he was painting them in detail. And he told us that it was Chocky who was doing it. Chocky would just take his hands and work them. He was painting as she saw. That was when we had to believe that something really weird was going on. I don't mean that those paintings you saw at the exhibition were Chocky's. She just taught him how to see, how to use his hands. She left him in the end. You heard about that?'

'Yes,' I said.

Matthew had been kidnapped. You'll have heard about that too. In the newspapers, on the television. 'Boy Artist Goes Missing' that sort of thing.

We cannot tell too much about that. The leader of the highbrow pundits and low-caste villains who abducted Matthew is a distinguished psychologist. He still practises in Harley Street. He is also a knight of the realm. David Gore sent his son to him on professional advice. It did not take long for the astute doctor to realise that the knowledge which Matthew revealed under hypnosis was extraordinary and potentially dangerous.

It had to do with cosmic energy, the very subject in which Chocky is now instructing Albertine. Cosmic energy – I don't really understand it, but it's all to do with protons and gravitons and pions and other 'ons' all bouncing off one another, repelling, attracting and what not. You'll find Albertine's explanation. – if you can call it an explanation – on page 35. The point seems to be – and it is accepted by the scientific establishment – that a lot of natural energy is being expended and that if we could harness just a minute part of it we would have boundless clean, safe energy for the rest of time. This is what Chocky, a petulant but otherwise benevolent being, wished to give to the world through Matthew.

The benefits to mankind of such a discovery are evident. The cost, however, to industries and economies founded upon fossil-fuels would be disastrous. That is why they kidnapped Matthew, pumped him full of drugs and interrogated him.

Luckily, Chocky had seen the danger. She left Matthew, but not before – so David Gore says – explaining her nature and her mission to him.

'She talked through Matthew at first, then she sort of materialised. I say "materialised", but in fact it was just her energy field that I could see – a sort of phosphorescent ectoplasm, a bright light spinning about an invisible centre. And she said – if "said" is the right word – I mean, I think that she spoke. I

22

heard this high, metallic sort of voice, and I think that I spoke back, though I'm not sure that I ever opened my mouth – she said that she had made a mistake in choosing Matthew. She had brought him nothing but danger. He could have been – would have been – mankind's greatest benefactor, the greatest scientist in history, but now, she said, she would work through a lot of different children, feed them knowledge piecemeal – rather like a cell system in a spy ring, you know? – so that no one of them possessed all the knowledge, so that the whole world might share it.

'So she left. That was when Matthew started to paint these views of windmills and of distant countries. Chocky's other children were reaching him, sharing their thoughts with him. The windmill was the Meyers' windmill. He drew it again and again in precise detail. Albertine and he were drawn together by their telepathy, but there are others, elsewhere in the world, who are being led and guided by Chocky. I don't even know whether they are aware of it. Albertine wasn't. Not for ages. Chocky whispers nowadays instead of shouting.'

David Gore is lean and fit. He has dark curly hair. It is beginning to turn grey, but he is obviously older than he looks. I have never seen him dressed other than casually. I rather like him. He is easy to talk to.

At the time, I admit, I was sceptical. I had only just started to research this story. I recorded the interview on my portable tape recorder. Doubt is evident in my voice as I asked his opinion.

'Are you trying to tell me . . . I don't know, it's a fascinating idea, but . . . are we to assume that other prodigious geniuses – Mozart, Rimbaud, for example,

Chatterton, people like that – that they all had their Chockys?'

'Dunno,' Gore shrugged. 'It's possible. I mean, they didn't invent their stuff. Ask any good artist. He'll always tell you. He's a cipher. Things come from somewhere and sort of flow through him. All that he can do is to be well trained, prepared, so that he will be an efficient cipher. Maybe there have always been Chockys or intelligences like Chocky, whispering in the ears of the most gifted people.'

The tape tells me that I said, 'Maybe. It's possible. I suppose . . .'

'So where are your sister and mother?' Albertine slumps down into a wicker chair in the corner.

'They're still up in Hindmere.' Matthew kneels beside her. 'Polly's got to go to school, you know. A friend of Dad's let us have the studio just while we were getting ready for the show.'

'I don't think there's a single picture unsold.'

'No. It's going well. I've got one for you.'

'I know. It's lovely.'

'Oh.' Matthew offers her a bowl of olives.

The crowds are thinning now. Mrs Gibson waggles her fingers at Matthew from the door and calls, 'Bye-bye!'

'Yes,' she says, 'I'm pretty certain we'll get it. I've got to write a report. Chocky'll help me. Then we'll be able to get on with the work.'

'How long will it take to get the money?'

'A month. No more, with luck.' She looks down at Matthew where he kneels at her feet. He gazes out through the plate glass windows. It is dark now. 'Are you OK, Matthew?' she asks.

'Yup. Fine.'

24

'Do you wish you were back with us, involved in it all again?'

'No.' Matthew does not look at her. 'No. I couldn't cope with all this. Maths and so on. It's not my thing. It nearly drove me mad the first time. Anyhow, I am still involved, sort of. It's just . . . Sometimes I miss having Chocky there, you know?'

'I know. But she always is there really. You just need to need her badly enough and she'll be there. You're her oldest friend, her first friend. She knows you better than me. Sometimes I think she only uses me because I'm bright in the right field.'

'I still *feel* that she's there.'

'She is.' Albertine touches his shoulder lightly. 'You can feel it, can't you?'

'Yes.' Matthew grins and jumps to his feet. 'Course I can. Just being silly. Come on. I'll give you that picture . . .'

'What, Chocky? No. I think they're all part of the same radio telescope. They're looking at the stars, of course. Well, I don't know. Yes, well, it may look primitive to you, but it's nearly the latest thing in these parts . . .'

In jeans and tee-shirt and flip-flop sandals, Albertine strolls across the long grass towards the row of parabolic dishes that scan the sky. This is the Cambridge radio telescope.

'No,' she shakes her head. Her sandals now drag on tarmac. 'No, I don't know, Chocky! It's not my field. You know that. You must have worked it out, haven't you? Good. OK, so children have toys like this in your . . .'

'What are you doing here, young lady?' demands a woman's voice. Albertine turns and counters.

'Do you use this telescope?'

'Of course. I am Beatrice Liddle. *Doctor* Beatrice Liddle. I'm an astronomer. That's what I am doing here. Which brings us back to my original question – what are *you* doing here?'

'I'm hoping to do some research.'

'You-ou?' A disbelieving laugh divides the word. 'Research? Into what – for the Lord's sake?'

'Cosmic energy,' Albertine says stolidly, 'and gravitational waves.'

'Science fiction stuff, eh?'

'No. Just science.'

'What makes you think that either of them exists?'

'I know . . .' Albertine checks her impatient reply. 'I mean – that's why I want to research them. To find out.'

'Yes. Well.' Liddle starts up the steps to the big smoked glass doors. 'I just hope you're not planning to use this instrument.'

'No,' Albertine follows. She chooses her words carefully. 'I just thought that, if I'm going to be working in astrophysics, I ought to find out as much as I can about what other people are doing in the field.'

Liddle turns at the door. She nods. The taut line of her mouth softens. 'I suppose that's fair. As long as you don't interrupt or try to interfere with my work.'

'Would you tell me about it?' Albertine smiles ingratiatingly. 'Please?'

Liddle considers for a second. 'All right,' she nods, 'yes. Come on.'

She pushes through the door. She does not bother to hold it open for Albertine. It swings back. Albertine catches it. She has to push very hard.

'. . . our largest and highest resolution instrument,'

Liddle's voice echoes about the spotless entrance hall as though in a public swimming pool. 'It's a five kilometre Earth rotation synthesis radio telescope, consisting of four fixed and four moveable dishes on an east-west baseline.' She pushes the button by the lift.

Albertine catches up as fast as she can. Her flip-flops flip and flop. With the benefit of the echo, they make a slovenly counterpoint to the crisp, efficient clipping of Liddle's footfalls.

'Why synthesis?' Albertine pants.

'Because it synthesises the image that we would have obtained with one very large dish, or rather, the computer does, when all the signals are fed into it over a period of time.'

The lift arrives. The door hisses open. Liddle steps in and turns on her heel like a sentry. She clutches her papers to her chest. She does not look at Albertine.

'So the whole thing's controlled by a computer, is it?'

'Of course,' Liddle hums. 'The computer steers the instrument and processes all the signals. Once it's set up and programmed, we can just leave it to get on with it. Sometimes no one comes near it for days.'

The life inhales deeply, stops and sighs. Liddle strides from it into the control room. Everything here is white, save the keys on the vast computer console.

Albertine says, 'I don't know, I'll ask.'

'What?' Liddle snaps over her shoulder.

'Nothing. Sorry. Just thinking aloud again . . .'

'Lord's sakes, girl. Surely you've passed the stage of imaginary companions by now . . .'

It is dark now. In the Meyers' house on Chaucer

27

Road, Albertine is working late. A single fringed glass lamp hangs over the desk. It shifts a little in a draught. The dusty light that it casts rocks from side to side. It's like being on a ship. Albertine catches herself swaying in time with it. She half-smiles, and stops herself. Outside, a big wind scampers around the house. It punches at the doors and rattles the window panes.

At last, she slaps down her pen and stretches. 'Oh, Chocky,' she creaks. 'That'll have to do for now. I'm exhausted . . . eyes are going all wonky . . . Thank you. It's very interesting. I'm enjoying it. The spirit is willing enough, but the flesh, I'm afraid, is weak . . .' She smiles. 'Yes,' she says.

She places a large paperweight on her work and stands. She stretches again. She walks in short, unsteady steps to the door.

At the foot of the stairs, she stops, closes her eyes and groans, 'Yes?' then 'Yes?' then, 'Chocky, I'm exhausted. I want to go to bed. The last thing I need is to hear you bragging about how primitive our telescopes are compared to yours. I know you think that we're little better than cavemen, but . . . Still, what?' Her eyes open. 'Do you think so? It might work. I suppose, but your planet is such a long way away . . . Yes, all I'd have to do would be to get into the computer that controls the telescope. I could do it through the phone line if I knew the phone number and the computer code . . . You did?' she is suddenly awake and excited. 'OK, I'll go downstairs and have a go!'

She opens the door under the stairs and switches on the light. She almost skips down the steps into the cellar. She flicks another switch. Two long strip-lights buzz and blink at her. She blinks back.

The usual lumber, toolkits, hammers, nails, picture frames, old albums, teachests and trunks, have been pushed back into the far corner. Now the centre of the room is sparsely but functionally furnished and scrupulously clean. A large formica-topped table stands in the very middle. There are two grey filing cabinets and two gate-backed chairs. Two Commodore Amiga keyboards lie on a sloping shelf along the left hand wall, their VDU's immediately above them.

Albertine sits at the nearest keyboard and flicks more switches. The VDU lights up. She reaches over to plug her terminal into the telephone system, then sits poised, her fingers curled above the keyboard. 'OK, Chocky,' she whispers, 'what is it? Six, zero, two, nine, zero. Right. And the code? Nine, six, one, four, three . . . two. Got it. And . . .'

The printer hums for a couple of seconds, then chatters.

'We're in, Chocky!' Albertine grins. 'Now what?'

She listens and nods. 'Brilliant! OK, but Chocky, can you do this for me? I mean, rather than you dictating the programme to me, could I think of nothing and let you take over? I'm tired. I might make mistakes. OK? Great . . .'

Albertine close her eyes and rests her fingers lightly on the keyboard. She lets out a deep sigh. Suddenly, her fingers are moving, flickering at dazzling speed across the keys. They move faster than those of any shorthand typist, faster than those of a virtuoso pianist, until the tap tap tap becomes just one continuous sound, like the screech of a fishing reel.

And a mile and a half away the enormous dishes of the telescope groan as they are awoken and shift slowly in obedience to their new controllers.

Chapter three

Albertine does not like the telephone. She prefers to write. I have only met her once in person, but she has sent me a lot of letters since I started to work on this book. She writes in a curiously elegant hand for one so rational and precise.

'I know I shouldn't have done it,' she wrote in her second letter (September 12th), 'but I was just so excited at the prospect of finding Chocky's home planet. You see, because only Chocky's mind travels – and travels is the wrong word, because it doesn't actually pass other points in order to reach us – she has no points of reference with which to identify her planet from earth. She can't say, as it were, "Go down to the Post Office and turn right," because she hasn't passed the Post Office to get here. Her mind has come direct to mine. Do you see? So the idea of being able to locate a planet with intelligent life was too exciting, too important to pass up.

'That's the trouble with knowledge, isn't it? It's good to seek it, and you come to want it so desperately, but sometimes you want it so badly that the rules seem unimportant. The end justifies the means. And its terribly difficult to decide just when you say, "No, I won't seek knowledge any further because I'd have to break the rules". . .

'Sorry. I'm almost as bad with letters as I am on the telephone. I'm not very good at expressing my thoughts clearly in language . . .'

*

'Fascinating!' Professor Ferris hits the desktop with Albertine's bulky report. 'Absolutely fascinating. Quite extraordinary.'

There are dark rings under Albertine's eyes. Her shoulders sag. Chocky has kept her up until three, four in the morning for the past fifteen days, teaching, explaining, dictating, but at Ferris' words she looks up and her blue-grey eyes flash.

Her father growls contentedly. He leans forward, his forearms on his knees.

Down in Hindmere, in Sussex, Matthew stops raking the lawn and grins. He stands there for a minute or two, just leaning on the rake and listening.

'So you think it's an acceptable subject for research, Professor?' Meyer asks.

'Speaking for myself,' Ferris paces back and forth past the window, his hands behind his back, 'speaking for myself, I have no doubts. No doubts whatsoever.'

'Thank you,' says Albertine.

'Ah, but,' Ferris wags a finger, 'you mustn't count your chickens, my dear. I am not the only person that you have to convince. There is a committee. Isn't there always a committee? You must remember that money is short, so there are only a limited number of projects that we can afford to finance.'

'Yes, yes,' Meyer says testily, 'we know all this, but it must be obvious that this work is important – uniquely important.'

'Ah, yes, Meyer,' Ferris sings, 'that's what everybody says, "My work is important". And everybody is quite right, but we can't give grants to all of them. And anyhow, most of our funds for the coming year are already spoken for. There is in fact

31

only one grant still available.'

'Oh, that's all right, then,' says Albertine blithely. 'As long as there is one available.'

'Yes, my dear, but you are not the only candidate. There is at least one other very worthy applicant that I know of.'

'Oh, who's that?'

'Beatrice Liddle.'

'Dr Liddle?' Albertine frowns. 'The astronomer?'

'That's right. You know her?'

'We've met.'

'Then you'll know how exciting she thinks her work is.'

'That's all very well, Professor,' Meyer says smoothly, 'but no matter how interesting it may be, it can't be as important as Albertine's. I mean – what is it, anyhow?'

Ferris regards him with amused exasperation. 'She is investigating a new binary star, Meyer.'

'Well, there you are.' Meyer waves aside universes in one flap of the hand. 'And we are talking about the discovery of an entirely new form of energy. Boundless, infinite energy. It goes without saying...'

Ferris is suddenly the teacher again. He leans forward on his fists and looks up at Meyer over his bifocals. 'What we are talking about,' he interrupts, 'is the *search* for boundless energy, which is hardly the same thing, is it? Theories are one thing, proof is quite another...'

Someone hammers hard on the panelled door. Ferris frowns and breaks off. 'Come,' he calls dubiously.

The door swings inward and stays open. Liddle marches in. Her chest is puffed out, her fists clenched at her sides. A hank of hair hangs in a streak across her forehead. 'Professor Ferris!' she announces.

Ferris looks startled. 'Um, Dr Liddle,' he says mildly, 'what exactly are you doing here?'

'Someone has interfered with my program!' She booms out the words as though pounding a kettledrum. 'Someone has destroyed weeks of hard work!'

'How very tiresome for you. But I really don't see what I'm . . .'

'Tiresome! Is that all you can say? It's more than tiresome, Professor, it's criminal vandalism!'

'Yes, yes,' Ferris pats down the air, 'quite so . . .'

'Weeks of work! The telescope realigned on an entirely new heading! Intellectual vandalism! Someone . . .' she glares at Albertine and speaks through clenched teeth. 'Someone has broken into the computer and played games with the radio telescope!'

Pink spots grow on Albertine's cheeks. Her father watches Liddle over his shoulder with undisguised vexation. Ferris soothes, 'Honestly, Dr Little . . . some other time . . .'

Liddle takes a deep breath. She trembles. Her hands open and clench, open and clench. 'This is the perfect time,' she interrupts. 'I have racked my brain to think who could have done this thing, and then I realised. I caught her snooping around the observatory a fortnight ago. I was even foolish enough to show her round. *Is that not so, Miss Infant Prodigy?*'

All eyes now turn to Albertine. 'Do you know something about this, my dear?' Ferris asks softly.

'Um . . .'

'Of course she doesn't,' Meyer snaps, 'How could she?'

'Very easily, I'm sure,' says Liddle.

'Albertine?' Ferris urges.

'Yes.' Albertine looks down at her hands. 'I'm sorry.'

'Albertine!'

'Oh, dear.'

'Ha! I knew it! Do you realise what you have done to my program? Have you any idea? Have you?'

'I was – I was always very careful to put everything back where it was,' she says in a small voice. Her hand rests lightly on her father's sleeve.

'And what use do you think that is, you little fool?' Liddle barks. 'That telescope is set on a continuous program. It has to go on without any interruptions for weeks on end.'

Albertine stands and faces Liddle. Tears burn her eyes. 'I'm very, very sorry,' she gulps. 'I didn't realise.'

'It's too late to be sorry,' Liddle scowls, 'the damage is done. I'll have to start all over again.'

'I cannot imagine what came over you, Albertine,' Meyer too stands. 'I am very disappointed ... dismayed.'

Albertine sniffs once and bites her lower lip. 'I'm sorry. I promise I won't do it again.'

'There, now.' Ferris comes round the desk and puts his arm around Albertine's shoulders. She stands stiffly to attention, but her lower lip trembles. 'You have had an apology and a promise, Dr Liddle. I think perhaps we should put it down to – shall we say youthful indiscretion? – and leave the matter there. Hmmm?'

Liddle gnaws on her lip for a second, then sighs. 'Very well, I suppose so.'

'Excellent. Now, will you have some coffee?'

'No, thank you. I have a great deal of work to do. An enormous amount of work. Good morning.' She returns to the sentry routine, swivels round on her heel and marches briskly from the room. She leaves the door open behind her. They can hear her footfalls overtaking one another as they recede down the corridor.

Ferris lopes over to close the door. Meyer slumps down on to the sofa again. 'Albertine, how could you?'

Albertine studies her shoes a little more.

'Ah, well,' Ferris smiles, 'I daresay it was just curiosity. And no permanent harm done, so let's leave it at that, shall we? We have more important things to discuss. First, I suggest that we have this report of yours published. Any objections?'

Albertine shakes her head. Meyer says, 'Of course not.'

'Good. Leave that to me, then. And you ought to give a public lecture on it. I'll see what I can arrange.'

'Me? Lecture?' Albertine at last looks up.

'Yes,' says Ferris.

'Yes,' says Meyer.

'The term "Cosmic Ray" is applied to elementary particles, usually protons, electrons or the nuclei of atoms, which travel through space at a velocity close to the speed of light. Some ninety per cent of the particles are protons, the nuclei of hydrogen atoms. Most of the rest are alpha-particles, the nuclei of helium atoms.

'The bulk of the particles have energies around 10^8 to 10^9 electron volts, but many particles have much greater energies. Some of them reach 10^{20} electron volts, many orders of magnitude greater than can be generated by particle accelerators in terrestrial laboratories. The energy contained in a single cosmic ray proton of this type is at least 16 Joules, which would be enough to lift a heavy book, for example, several centimetres into the air . . .'

Her confidence grows as she speaks. She faltered and her voice quavered at the outset, but now the practised words trip readily from her tongue. She has leisure to look about the beautiful, high-vaulted Royal Institution lecture theatre. Amidst the hundreds of unfamiliar faces beneath the dais, she can pick out some which she recognises. Ferris is there with her father. Professors Wade and Draycott of her Faculty sit behind them. She has not yet located Matthew and David Gore, but she knows that they are there.

'. . . When high-speed cosmic ray protons collide with hydrogen atoms in the interstellar medium, nuclear reactions take place between them and a number of pions are created. These pions are unstable, and decay almost immediately to produce a pair of gamma rays, with an energy of about 100 mega electron volts each, which can pass right across the galaxy with almost no hindrance from the interstellar medium . . .'

She pauses for a second. She scans the ranked seats. David Gore, sitting high up in the second row from the back suddenly hears whispering from the seat on his left. He turns to look at his son. 'Up here,' Matthew is saying, 'Yes. I can hear you perfectly. You're doing fine . . .'

A fat, balding man in front of Matthew turns and hushes him. Gore catches Matthew's eye and grins.

'Equating this to a gravitational-wave force delta F, the electro-magnetic noise in gravitationl-wave units is therefore . . .'

She turns. She has to stand on tiptoe to write on the

36

blackboard behind her. The chalk cracks on the first stroke. Very calmly, she picks up another stick and writes:

$$^hEM = \bar{3} \times 10^{-17}\ \frac{L(d\ E_z/dz)}{0.004mVm^{-1}}\ \frac{30mHz^2}{f}\ \frac{V_o}{1V}$$

She underlines it with a shriek.

She dusts her hands and turns back to the audience.

In the back row, just two along to Matthew's right, is a woman. She wears a stern, smart black suit and, this time, a white shirt with a high collar. Her pale reddish brown hair is tight set beneath a glistening layer of laquer, sixties style.

She was at Matthew's exhibition. She admired Matthew's paintings. She called herself Pru Gibson. Mrs Gibson.

She watches both Matthew and Albertine. When Matthew whispered to Albertine a few minutes ago, she nodded and scribbled something on the small pad in her lap.

Albertine winds up: 'The aim of these experiments will be to identify and eventually to collect gravitational waves from black hole events in galactic nuclei and stellar collapses, which are both impulsive sources, and continous sources such as binary stars and pulsars in the Crab Nebula. Thank you.'

She sits down quickly. There is silence in the auditorium for at least five seconds, then Ferris claps. Meyer follows suit and suddenly a big explosion of applause shakes the walls of the old theatre and makes the boards of the dais hum. Matthew stands and claps with his hands above his head. Gibson watches him and smiles.

The applause at last dies down.

There's one person in that lecture theatre whom we cannot see. She is sitting too far from Matthew, too far from the people whom Albertine looks down upon.

Because we cannot see her I do not know whether Beatrice Liddle is scowling or smiling as the applause bursts over Albertine like a fireball.

I only know that she is there because she told me so. 'I mean,' she said, 'that lecture of hers was good in its way. Showy but without substance, that's how I saw it at the time. I was wrong, as it happens, but I didn't know that then. A lot of my peers agreed with me, as a matter of fact. It all looked so certain, so glib. Stunningly clever, of course, but – well, flashy, specious, you know what I mean?'

'But I want you to *know* that I enjoyed your lecture *very* much!' Jean Wade talks like a grandmother's letter, all underlined words and exclamation marks, 'but I must say, I found it *rather theoretical*. This grant is essentially for *practical* work, you know. If we *should* decide to give the grant to you, do you *really* believe that you can achieve successful experiments?'

'Yes,' Albertine answers quietly. 'I do.'

She sits alone on a hard-backed chair in the middle of Ferris' room. Her hands are folded decorously in her lap, her knees tucked up under her chair.

This is an inquisition. Three distinguished scholars sit behind the desk. They lean on their blotters. Occasionally their eyes leave her as they jot down a note. Ferris is in the middle. Professor Wade, Albertine's tutor, a plump woman with salt and pepper hair, sits on his right. On his left, Professor Draycott leans forward and fires off questions like Jimmy Connors' volleys. Draycott has a lean and hungry look and crewcut colourless hair. He looks at his watch between questions.

'So!' he woofs. 'Fancy that, now. I wish I could be so certain of success everytime I start an experiment.'

'But . . .'

'Quite,' Ferris nods, ever the mediator. 'Surely you can only say that you hope that the experiments will succeed? Hmmm?'

'No.' Albertine shifts her legs. 'I know that they will.'

'Now, now.' Draycott glances at his watch. He has thin, very dry lips that hardly move as he speaks. 'That is arrogant nonsense, girl. Nobody can possibly say that. Quite absurd.'

Albertine is no diplomat. She dislikes Draycott, partly because of his vole's head, partly because of his eyebrows, which are paler than his hair, partly because of those thin lips. Principally because of his manners. 'I can,' she says.

'Albertine, *please*,' Ferris begs.

'I *admire* confidence,' Wade smiles, 'but you must beware of *over*-confidence, you know.'

Draycott says something like 'Pshaw!', then, 'Statements like that are irresponsible. Still,' he looks at his watch, 'nothing more than I'd expect from someone who would tamper with other people's work.'

'Sorry?' Wade turns to him, '*What's* that?'

'Oh, haven't heard, eh? About this girl getting into the radio telescope?'

'That incident was not to be talked about,' says Ferris firmly. 'Dr Liddle agreed.'

'Dr Liddle was beside herself with fury, and I can't say I blame her. Her whole program was ruined.'

'But *what* happened? What *did* she do?'

'I said I was sorry.' Albertine looks close to tears. 'She promised it was over . . .'

'Indeed she did,' says Ferris. 'In this very room.'

'But it's all *out* now, isn't it?' Wade nods sympathetically, 'So we might as *well* hear the whole story, dear.'

'This girl,' Draycott points, 'managed to make a connection with the computer controlling the big telescope and fed in her own program. She was using the telescope like some sort of expensive toy.'

'I wasn't! That's not fair!'

'Oh, *dear*,' Wade sighs. '*Not* the sort of behaviour one *expects* of a *research* fellow . . .'

'But precisely the sort of behaviour one would expect of an immature child,' Draycott sneers. 'How can we possibly even think of giving our one remaining research grant to somebody who can be so irresponsible?'

'Look – look . . .' Albertine blinks. She holds up a hand to quiet the storm. 'I wasn't playing. I was searching for a planet.'

'Not so difficult, I'd have thought. There are several billions of them, after all.'

'Not like this one.' There is a catch in Albertine's voice.

'Oh? So what's so special about this one, then? Inhabited or something?'

'If you must know,' Albertine snaps back, 'yes, it is!'

'Albertine . . .' Ferris rests his forehead in his open hand and moans, 'Oh, Albertine . . .'

Draycott barks, 'Wonderful! And I suppose you found this planet?'

Albertine's eyes swivel desperately from Draycott, who leans forward poised like a foxhound before its quarry, to Ferris, who now has both hands over his face, to Wade, who shakes her head very slowly. 'No!' she shakes. 'We didn't find that planet, but we did receive signals from other planets which these beings have colonised!'

'Little green men?' Draycott laughs. 'Eyes in the middle of their foreheads, I suppose?'

'No!' Albertine stands. 'It's not like that. We received signals from them!'

'*You* found intelligent life forms?' Draycott gasps between guffaws. '*You?* Something the world has been trying to do for centuries?'

'I *really* think we've heard *enough*, Albertine.' Wade draws one straight line across her pad.

'It's true!' Albertine steps forward. She hits the desk hard with her fist. Tears run down her red cheeks. 'You've got to believe me! I have a friend!'

'From outer space?'

'Yes!' She is almost doubled up now. She hits the desk again and again. 'Yes, yes, yes, yes, yes!!' A sob shakes her shoulders and she, like Ferris, covers her face with her hands. 'Oh, Chocky,' she hiccoughs, 'please, Chocky . . . please help me . . . *please!*'

And the laughter stops.

Chapter four

What happens now is difficult to explain simply because everyone sees it differently. Draycott refused to talk to me about it save to say, 'Some damned illusionist's trick or other. Seems to have conned poor old Ferris,' but also, 'Of course I didn't *see* anything. How could I? Just a trick of the light or something. Perfectly commonplace . . .'

Draycott is a creature of convention. What does not fit the patterns of received wisdom does not exist. Lots of people are like this. But the scientist who does not believe in magic is no true scientist.

When Captain Cook arrived for the first time in the Antipodes, the aboriginal fishermen did not see him. There he was, floating by in his vast galleon with huge sails and endless rigging and guns and so on, and the fishermen were just feet away. But they looked at this enormous technological marvel and, because it was so far removed from anything that they had ever known before, they did not see it. It was beyond their ken, so it did not exist.

There are a lot of scientists and doctors like that. There will be a lot more if everyone learns their science through computers. I know that because Albertine told me so (October 13th) and she says that Chocky told her.

Ferris told me a different story. 'I looked up to see why the laughter had stopped. There was this high-pitched whine – no, not strictly a whine – more like the sound that a bell or a glass gives off after it has been struck, only whereas the peal of a bell diminishes, this sound swelled. The nearest approximation I can come to is the sound made by a wet finger running around a crystal glass – you know? – only infinitely stronger and more resonant.

'And suddenly above Albertine there was this light source. I don't know what colour it was precisely, because there was nothing – no *thing*, you understand me – there. It was like taking the light that comes off a lake – all the flashes and twinkles and all that, and removing the lake, or a diamond – only it was moving. So it was pink and purple and green and gold all at the same time. I don't know. And it spoke – or at least, there was sense in this crystal humming sound . . .'

'It was *quite* simple,' Jean Wade told me, 'and *quite* remarkable. This brilliant ball of *light* appeared – Albertine *tells* me that it is her friend's *energy field* . . .'

'But Professor Draycott told me that there was nothing there,' I told her. 'Just a reflection or something . . .'

'Oh, that's just *Wilfrid*. He's an old fool. Always *has* been as a matter of fact. I knew him *much* better in the *old* days, when he was still an old fool, but really *quite* attractive. If it was just a *reflection*, I'd like to know why his mouth dropped open and his eyes popped *clean* out of his head when he saw it, wouldn't you? No. There was this spinning *ball* of light and it said quite clearly – I *know* it's difficult to believe, but *really*, I am *not* the sort of woman who sees pink elephants, you know – it said, "I am Albertine's *friend*. My name is Chocky."'

*

'Oh, Chocky,' Albertine grins through her tears, 'I'm sorry. I messed it all up, didn't I?'

'It's an illusion,' Draycott recovers his breath. 'Some sort of conjuring trick!'

'I don't think so,' says Wade 'I really don't think so.'

I am not an illusion. I have come to help you.

'But, where have you come from – er, Chocky, is it?'

'It is.'

Draycott looks at his watch. 'He's talking to it now!' he shrieks. 'He's off his head! Ha! I always knew he was unstable, of course, but . . .'

'Oh, do be *quiet*, Wilfrid!' says Wade.

'What?'

'Do please shut *up*, you *silly* man!'

'But you – you're an astrophysicist! Jean – don't tell me you too . . . You can't take this tomfoolery seriously!'

'Wilfrid,' Wade says calmly, 'if you *don't* shut up, I shall *strike* you very hard with this paperweight.'

'Well, you can stay and make fools of yourselves if you want to.' Draycott stands. He picks up his papers and pushes back the chair. 'But I am not staying here to be made a fool of by this – this . . .' he clicks his fingers, 'this *chit*!' He strides around the desk, ducks apprehensively under Chocky's floating energy field and storms from the room.

'I *am* sorry about that,' Wade smiles up at Chocky.

I have come from a distant planet. Many parsecs away. So far away, I cannot begin to describe to you where it is.

'That's what we were doing with the radio telescope,' Albertine explains, 'trying to locate Chocky's home.'

Ferris nods. 'So what do you want from us?'

'*I do not want anything from you. I want to give you something.*'

'Good of you,' Ferris beams. 'But what?'

'*The secret of cosmic power. It is the duty of all intelligent life forms to help each other. More advanced intelligences such as my own must pass on their knowledge to lesser forms such as yours, so that you may develop and break out of your primitive technology.*'

'Primitive?' murmurs Wade.

'*Oh, yes. Your technology is extremely primitive. You have only recently learned to exploit the stored energy of your sun – for that is what all your fuels are. But soon you must break free of the closed circle of your sun-based economy. You will need cosmic energy. It is a source of infinite power, and so of infinite possibilities . . . I intend to explain all of this to you. Cosmic energy costs nothing. It is freely available and unlimited. It can never be used up. It will last as long as the universe itself . . .*'

'It's a dream,' whispers Wade, '*the* dream . . .'

'The gateway to the golden age,' Ferris murmurs.

'*Albertine is your key to that gateway. I am working through her. But you must provide her with the facilities that she needs. You must!*'

'We will,' says Ferris.

'Of course we will,' Wade nods.

'*Look after her. Keep her safe. Tell no one what she is really doing until she has achieved my purpose.*'

'I give you my word,' says Ferris.

'And I mine. We promise.'

'*That is good. I thank you. Goodbye.*'

'There was a noise like the sea when it rushes back, sucking up pebbles,' said Wade. 'A hushing sort of sound. And the light faded in stages like an echo.

And suddenly we looked around and everything seemed very dark and very unfamiliar. Even simple everyday things seemed odd.'

And Ferris turns to Wade. Both smile. He holds out his hand to Albertine. 'My dear,' he says, 'you have your grant . . .'

'Yes, yes . . .' Ferris nods as he scans the list. 'This doesn't look too horrendous. And you really think that this place will be sufficient, hmm?' He looks dubiously around the Meyers' drawing-room.

'Well, yes,' Meyer makes a large gesture with his cigar-case hand. 'It's essential for us to have somewhere safe and above all, somewhere private. The press can't bother us too much here, and we're well out of the way. I'll show you where the work can be done.' He takes the professor's arm. 'Come with me . . .'

Together they go down to the cellar where Albertine sits tapping at her computer keyboard. She stands as they enter, but Ferris waves her back into her seat. 'Ah, yes. Yes, I think you have room enough down here,' Ferris bleats. 'Excellent. That will be another economy for the university. Very satisfactory. Now, Albertine, of course, will be reporting to me in the end, but she'll need a supervisor for the project.'

'My father can do that,' says Albertine, without missing a beat.

'That would be somewhat unusual, you know.'

'The fewer outsiders the better,' says Meyer conspiratorially.

'Yes, yes, I suppose you're right. I dare say I can persuade the other members of the board to agree with that, if I assume final responsibility.'

'Good.'

'Which brings us to the question of staff. You'll need some good research assistants.'

'We can find those.' Albertine stops typing and turns in her chair. 'It's all right.'

'You?' Ferris' eyebrows rise. 'But my dear, how would you know where to find the right people in this field?'

'Chocky will know,' she says simply.

'Ah, yes,' Ferris nods, 'Chocky. Of course.'

'Don't worry, Professor,' Meyer reassures him, 'it'll be all right. I promise you.'

'Yes. I know,' says Ferris unhappily. 'I believe you, but it's a matter of persuading others . . .'

'And they'll all be young people like me.' Albertine returns to her keyboard.

'Young people?' Ferris starts. 'You mean *children*?'

'That's right,' she beams.

'Oh, no, no, no, no, no, that's just not possible.' He slumps down into the other chair and smooths back the hair above his ears with the heel of his hand. 'I mean, to start off with, there simply cannot be others like you. You are a unique exception.'

'She is indeed an exception,' Meyer agrees. 'But not unique. There are others. Not quite as brilliant, perhaps, but they exist.'

'No,' Ferris' hands flap desperately and slap down on his thighs. 'I'm sorry, but no. I really cannot agree to that. I mean, a major research project, all run by children? We'd be the laughing stock of the university – of the entire academic world!'

'Oh, no!' Albertine freezes. Her hands remain just above the keys. 'But what will Chocky say?'

'It's – it's not here now, then?' Ferris glances nervously around the room.

'No,' Albertine turns her chair again. 'No, she's with somebody else at the moment. She can't be with me all the time.'

'No, no, of course.' Ferris shakes his head. 'But – children! We can't. It's simply not possible.'

'I'll tell you what!' In an uncharacteristic gesture of bonhomie, Meyer slaps Ferris' shoulder. 'Leave it for now, Professor. Keep an open mind about it. But come to tea with us on Sunday. There's somebody I'd like you to meet.' He looks across to Albertine. 'Sunday will be all right, won't it?'

She closes her eyes and links her fingers. She takes a deep breath. The two men wait for a minute, maybe more, then Albertine smiles. 'Yes,' she says, 'Sunday's fine. Well done, Daddy.' She reaches up to take her father's hand. 'That's a brilliant idea.'

Matthew paints with slow, methodical dabs and strokes of the brush. Like the old masters, he is working up through pure white on a huge canvas. This painting is very different from those at the exhibition. The colours are vivid and strong. From the sketches on the wall it is clear that the whole picture will soon be filled with human figures, buildings and flowers.

He stands in his studio – a sunny, white extension to his parents' Hindmere home. A bee buzzes around his head as he paints.

'That's going well, old boy.' David Gore looks over his son's shoulder. Matthew jumps.

'Yes,' Matthew sighs and lays down his palette, 'it's OK, but it's still not quite what's in my head. I need to improve my technique with oils.'

'Well, you might just have the opportunity to do that.' Paper rustles at Matthew's elbow.

'Why? What is it?'

48

'Oh, nothing much. Just turns out that the principal of the Metropolitan Academy in New York was at your exhibition, that's all, and on the strength of what he saw, he's offering you a Kennedy scholarship to study painting there. That's all. Sorry if I disturbed you . . .'

'What?' Matthew grins. 'New York? Hey, that sounds really exciting.'

'Thought you'd think so. Look, read it.'

Matthew wipes his hands on a filthy old rag and takes the letter.

'They'll arrange your ordinary schooling, as you see,' Gore goes on. And my boss has arranged an exchange for me with the firm's New York office. If you're happy about the idea, it's all settled.'

'It's amazing!' Matthew beams as he comes to the end of the letter, 'It's a really great opportunity.' Then, 'Hold on, Dad.'

Gore stands still, his hands on his hips, and waits, almost embarrassed, for a minute or so while Matthew concentrates. At last his son looks up and him and smiles happily.

'Albertine be OK while you're away?' Gore asks.

'Yes,' Matthew nods, 'she's delighted. But will Sunday be OK, Dad?'

'OK for what?'

'Oh, sorry. To go up to Cambridge for tea. Say good-bye and things.'

'Yes,' Gore considers, 'yes, I think so. Good idea. Perfect weather for a stroll along the backs. You've never been there, have you? Properly, I mean.'

'No,' says Matthew, 'I'd like to. It looks lovely. They want me to bring my oboe with me. She didn't tell me why.' He flaps with the letter at the persistent bee . . . 'Oh, go away!'

*

They wave goodbye to Ferris from the doorstep as his taxi moves away. No sooner is he gone than Albertine clutches her father's sleeve. 'Daddy, Matthew's got a Kennedy scholarship to New York, the Metropolitan Academy, and all his family is going too, isn't it great, and he'll come on Sunday to say good-bye and they'll be off in just a couple of weeks and he's just been stung by a bee.'

'Oh,' says Meyer drily, 'good. Except, of course, for the bee. That is unfortunate. Quite extraordinary,' he mumbles as he shuts the door and heads off towards the living-room. 'Otherwise intelligent daughter . . . incapable of constructing a coherent English sentence . . .'

In inexpert hands, the oboe can be a harsh instrument. It can shriek like chalk on a blackboard. It can honk like a frightened duck. But that Sunday in the Meyer's back garden, his hair still wet after a swim in Byron's Pool, Matthew makes his oboe sing. He plays a piece by Julia Usher called, punningly, *A Reed in the Wind*. It is a complex modern piece in which each of the movements is named after a famous wind: Zephyrus, Mistral and so on.

The theme is perfectly suited to the instrument, for nothing is reedier or wilder than the pure wail of the oboe.

Ferris sits on the rug, his long legs outstretched before him. He is entranced. His eyes are closed. He nods, approving, conducting with his head. Beside him, her legs tucked up beneath her, Albertine smiles happily as she watches Matthew play. Occasionally she reaches over to take another strawberry from the ruins of tea which lie scattered on the rug. Gore lies on his side, his head propped up on one hand. He languorously enjoys the whole experience, the melding of music and birdsong and sunshine. As for Meyer, he sits crosslegged and frowns deeply. The music for him is a pleasing problem, not unlike a crossword puzzle for you or me. He is trying to work it out.

Matthew finally removes the reed from his lips, shrugs, sits down and takes a slice of lemon cake.

'Bravo!' Ferris claps, 'Oh, bravo, young man!'

'Very good, Matthew.' Meyer's tone is that of a committee awarding some mark of approval. 'A most interesting piece.'

'Oh, Matthew, that was super!' Albertine has risen to her knees to applaud.

Gore contents himself with a secret smile to his son. 'Well done, old boy.'

'I do congratulate you.' Ferris pats Matthew's shoulder. 'Really. The oboe is a notoriously difficult instrument. It must have taken enormous dedication to reach such a standard.'

Matthew wipes crumbs from the corner of his mouth. He licks his fingers, swallows. 'Not really, Professor. I just play for fun.'

'Fun!' Ferris chuckles. 'Well, your enjoyment certainly shows, but you must have put in a great deal of long, hard work. How old were you when you started?'

'Thirteen.'

'Thirteen?' Ferris smiles, but the smile suddenly vanishes and his brow wrinkles. 'Hold on. That's not possible. You can't be much more than that now.'

'No. I'm only fourteen. Is there any more iced coffee, Albertine?'

'It's true,' Gore nods at the Professor. 'He's fourteen and three months. I bought him that instrument just six, seven months ago. He'd never played it before.'

'It's – it's extraordinary . . .' Ferris drinks from his empty teacup. He does not seem to notice that it is empty. It rattles as he lays it back in the saucer. 'It must be in the blood – in the genes, I should say. Are all your family such good musicians, young man?'

Matthew's mouth is full of scone, strawberry jam and clotted cream. He shakes his head. His eyes twinkle as they catch Albertine's.

'No,' says Gore, 'he's the only one of us who can play a note.'

Ferris is a little lost. He shakes his head again and again. He looks from the Gores to the Meyers, suspecting some sort of trickery. 'But such talent! And – and you've *no* idea where you get it from?'

'Oh, yes,' says Meyer, 'oh, yes, I think we all know that, don't we Matthew?'

'Yes, it's perfectly simple, Professor, really.'

All four are now smiling at one another. Ferris alone frowns.

'I think we should put the poor Professor out of his misery,' Gore grins.

'Remember Chocky?' says Albertine.

'Chocky?' he gazes at Matthew. 'You mean, you, too?'

Matthew nods.

'Matthew was the first of Chocky's children,' Meyer explains.

'So – so you mean this is the person you want to work with you, Albertine?'

'Oh, no. Matthew's work is in art. He's going to New York on a Kennedy scholarship.'

'You see,' says Matthew, 'Chocky says that it's just as important that people should see things properly as that they should be shown what to see. That's my job in my painting.'

'This,' says Ferris, 'is all getting a little too much for me.'

'You see,' Albertine urges, 'Chocky has found some others who are especially good at science and mathematics. They are the ones who will be helping me.'

'Yes, that's all very well, Albertine. I see that. But what in heaven's name do we tell people. How are we going to explain turning an expensive research programme over to children, no matter how talented?'

'Well, we've been thinking about that, Professor,' Meyer smiles, 'and I think we may have come up with a solution. Why don't we say that it's a special research programme into gifted children conducted by the faculty?'

'Gifted children?' sings Ferris. 'Hmm. Yes. Yes, I like it. After all,' he grins, 'I suppose it's basically true.'

'It would have the added advantage, of course, of helping to persuade the parents to let their children come here. They may not yet know, you see, that Chocky is guiding them.'

'I think,' says Ferris, 'that we might just get away with it.'

Chapter five

It is September. The wind has taken on an edge. The sunny days are fewer. Albertine hardly notices. From morning till night, she has been busy in the cellar, setting up the new equipment and continuing her work with Chocky. Chocky seldom lets up.

Her father too has been busy. When not helping her in the practical aspects of her work, he has been writing letters, making telephone calls. Chocky's children have been identified. That was the easiest part of the enterprise. Since then, there have been parents to appease, insurance and travel arrangements to be organised, rooms in the house to be prepared for each of them.

Today at last – September 20th – Meyer is to spend the day at Heathrow airport. Su Lin, a thirteen-year-old Chinese girl, arrived on a flight from Hong Kong at seven-thirty this morning. Mike, a black American, flies in from Boston at four o'clock this evening – just one and a half hours from now.

Albertine has put flowers in their rooms and has prepared their places in the basement. They have a new, more capacious computer with which to work. Because of the telepathy which, Chocky assures her, will exist between them, they do not need separate systems. All four keyboards serve one central console. Albertine has just settled down to program in new data, which Chocky dictates to her, when the doorbell rings.

She curses. 'Sorry, Chocky, hold on a second.'

She trots up the stairs and into the hall. University full-term has begun. It is probably some keen politico student asking for funds for this or that cause.

She opens the front door and peers out. It has been raining. The gleaming pavements still seem to spit back at the sky. A little, plump man stands on the steps. He looks vaguely familiar, but it's difficult to recognise anyone under a dripping trilby. Behind him, in a long, blue car, another man sits waiting in the passenger seat.

'Yes?' says Albertine.

'Good morning.' The plump man touches his hat but does not remove it. 'Miss Meyer, as I recall?'

'Yes, that's right. Who are you?'

'Is your dad in?'

'No, I'm afraid not. Who are you?'

'Perhaps I could have a word with you about certain rumours I've heard . . .' He signals to the man in the car. There is a flash, a click, a whirring sound, a flash, a click, a whirring sound. And again. And again. 'Bolus. *The Sun*, you remember?'

'Oh, no!' Albertine steps back and slams the door, but too late. The flashes still circle behind her closed eyelids as wearily she returns to her work.

'*Reclusive child genius* is the caption,' Meyer reads bitterly. 'God, these gutter-rats! Who tipped them off?'

'It's a terrible picture,' says Albertine. 'Makes me look daft.'

'It's not that bad,' says Su Lin. All three children crowd around Meyer at the breakfast table as he reads:

'"Fourteen-year-old child genius Albertine Meyer, who astonished the world by coming out top in

55

Cambridge tripos exams after only one year, now has company. The university is starting a hush-hush research programme into gifted children. So far, two other intellectual whizz-kids have joined Albertine – Su Lin Chang from Hong Kong and Mike Harley from Boston, USA . . ." and so it goes on.' Meyer throws down the paper. 'Speculation, but well-informed speculation. Where the devil did they get that stuff?'

'Hey! Whaddya know!' Mike whoops. 'One day in this country and already we're famous!'

'More's the pity,' Meyer growls.

'Don't worry, Daddy. As long as they don't know about Chocky, or what we're really doing here. Matter of fact, we should be quite pleased. They've swallowed the "Research into gifted children" hook, line and sinker.'

'Mmm, I still don't like it. I don't like anything that draws attention to us. Still. Too late to worry now. Come on, all of you. It's getting late. Sit down and have some breakfast. We must get down to work.'

'Can we stop a little early this evening, Daddy?' Albertine asks as she sits and unfolds her napkin. 'I thought we could just take a walk along the backs. Show Su Lin and Mike some of their new home town?'

'Certainly,' Meyer nods. 'Good idea. But make sure I'm with you. I don't want you hounded by these darned muckrakers all the way.'

For a minute or two there is silence save for the usual breakfast noises. Suddenly Meyer looks up. There is just too much silence. No three healthy children can possibly sit still at a table without speaking for this long.

They are looking at one another, fixed as though in a freeze-frame. Albertine has her teacup halfway to her lips. Su Lin holds her butter charged knife just above her toast. Mike leans forward a little, his forearms resting on the table. Only their eyes move.

Then suddenly the stillness is broken. Su Lin lays down her knife, Albertine spills tea into her saucer. All three are laughing.

'Oh, no,' says Meyer, 'that is enough!'

'I'm sorry, Daddy,' Albertine pants between giggles. 'Mike was just telling us a joke.'

'I think we're going to have a new rule in this house.' Meyer folds his paper. 'When there are other people with you, you will always speak out loud. All right?'

'But it's so much quicker, Mr Meyer,' Su Lin protests. 'We just have to think.'

'And things like jokes are so much better because you see things rather than having to conjure up your own images through words.'

'Yes, I'm sure you're right. But you don't seem to understand that you're shutting other people out. It's like whispering. People are always going to feel nervous that you are talking about them or saying something that you wouldn't like them to hear. It creates unease.'

'You mean it's rude?' asks Mike.

'Exactly. That's what good manners means, isn't it? Putting people at their ease. If you make people uneasy, you're being bad mannered.'

'Yes,' Albertine nods, 'I see . . .'

The children look at one another again. They nod.

'Damn it, you're doing it again!' Meyer slurps his coffee, exasperated.

'I'm sorry,' Su Lin says sheepishly. 'We didn't

think. But we're all agreed. No telepathy in front of other people.'

'Good,' Meyer sighs. 'Just save it for your work or for emergencies.'

'We promise,' Albertine smiles, then, 'Uh, oh, telephone.'

'I'll get it.' Meyer strides over to the telephone on the wall. 'Hello. Meyer. Professor. Morning. Yes, we read it. What? Oh. Yes. Right away.' He slams down the telephone, as usual, without a goodbye. 'Something's wrong at the Faculty.' He reaches for a coat and shrugs it on. I'll see you later.'

The Faculty building is under siege. The pavement and the forecourt are already crowded with parents and with children. Meyer breathes, 'Oh, no!' as he parks his bicycle and begins to wade through the crowd towards the main door. Three times someone grabs his coat and asks, 'Are you one of the dons?' or 'Do you teach here?' He shakes his head and brushes off their hands. Twice, small children tug at his trouser legs. He just walks on, dragging them with him, and muttering, 'Excuse me, excuse me,' and 'Please get out of my way!'

At last he reaches the Porters' lodge. Three porters – usually a tough, unshakeable breed – stand at the gate. They are pink, sweating and flustered. Children paw their legs. Mothers pluck at their jackets.

'Yes, madam,' the head porter is saying, 'I'm sure he is quite brilliant, but I'm afraid you can't see Professor Ferris, and will you kindly inform your charming son that picking his nose and wiping his fingers on my trousers is not the sort of thing that we expect from our undergraduates and ... no, madam, will you *please* all go away!' He catches sight of Meyer and calls to him, 'Mr Meyer! Mr Meyer! You're to go straight up. You all right, sir?'

'Just about,' Meyer says grimly. 'Can you keep this mob at bay?'

'We'll cope, sir. Never saw anything like it in my life. Hope you can sort it out.'

'So do I.' Meyer takes a deep breath. 'All right. When you're ready. One, two, three . . . now!'

The head porter flings open the side gate. Meyer ducks and bolts through. A fat redheaded woman clings to his coat and tries to drag her equally red-headed child through the little gate. The porter grabs her unceremoniously by the scruff of the neck and drags her back. 'Not you, madam, thank you!'

The door slams. Meyer shakes his head and runs up the stairs to Ferris' office.

Ferris stands at the window. He gazes out on to the forecourt through net curtains. 'Ah, Meyer!' he greets him. 'We are besieged! It's like one of those dreadful, dreadful auditions you read about in the nastier newspapers. Every doting parent in Eastern England is here, convinced that his or her brat is a genius, and more will be on their way. It's only half-past ten and look at them! They'll be on their way from Yorkshire and from London and from the West Country . . . What are we going to *do*, Meyer? In addition to that loathsome newspaper, there was a report on the wireless this morning too . . .'

The telephone shrills. Ferris pounces on it as though he expects to find Superman at the other end of the line. 'Hello? Yes. *No*, madam. No, we are not looking or any more children. We have an abundance – a superabundance of children, thank you. No, madam. Good-bye!'

He replaces the receiver very carefully. It shrills

again as soon as it is laid down. He pulls back his hand as though burned.

'Excuse me, Professor,' says Meyer. He strides across to the desk, picks up the receiver and slams it down. He takes it off the hook again and leaves it lying on the desk.

'Thank you, Meyer,' says Ferris feebly, 'but we can't stay incommunicado forever. We've got to tell them something, but what?'

'I don't know. We can hardly tell them that it's all untrue, can we?'

'Hardly.'

'So why not simply take their names and addresses and particulars and say you'll get in touch with them?'

'Yes.' Ferris tugs at his hair. 'But what happens when I don't? They'll all come swarming back like flies when you've slapped them away.'

'Mmm,' Meyer pulls up a chair and rests his elbows on Ferris' desk. 'They do look somewhat determined.'

'Somewhat?' squeaks Ferris. 'Heaven save me from them. Oh, dear. It seemed such a good idea.'

'It was. It still is. I never thought . . .'

'I know. Neither did I.'

There is a long silence. The crowd outside bubbles and seethes. One child somewhere screams.

Suddenly Meyer clicks his fingers. 'I know!' he shifts forward and shoves out his jaw. 'I've got it! They want their children assessed. Very well, they will have their children assessed. We'll set them an examination!'

'Which they will all fail,' Ferris squeals with unexpected relish. He rubs his hands together. 'Yes! Excellent, Meyer! Get rid of the lot of them in one fell stroke. Splendid.'

'We run one risk, of course,' Meyer smiles.

'Hmm?'

'There might actually be a real genius among them.'

'We'll take that hurdle when we come to it,' Ferris beams contentedly. 'Right. When should this examination take place?'

'How about this afternoon?' Meyer shrugs. 'You and I can cobble together something suitably impossible by then.'

'Oh, yes,' Ferris says gleefully, 'I think so. Let's have it announced, shall we?'

Down in the cellar laboratory, the children sit at their separate keyboards. Chocky is speaking.

Our work will fall into three parts. First, we must construct an energy-collector, which will gather the energy from cosmic rays and muons. Second, we must build anti-gravity screens, which will operate with the energy collector. And when we have completed these two, I will show you how to harness the full power of the cosmos.

'Sorry, Chocky,' says Albertine, 'but why can't you tell us how it works first?'

You would not be able to understand it. It is difficult for human minds to make the giant leaps to such new concepts. That is why no one has discovered it before now. The capacity was there; the information was there; it is just such a different way of thinking . . .

'I hope we will be able to do it,' says Su Lin. 'It sounds very hard to me.'

'Me, too,' says Mike.

You will. I have chosen you three because you have special minds which are capable of accepting such changes. We shall proceed gradually, step by step. When we have finished, it will all seem obvious to you.

61

'Yeah, well,' Mike smiles, 'it still sounds like a lot of hard work.'

'Yes. There will be times when your minds will ache with pain. There will be times when you feel you can continue no longer. But you must. It will all be worth it in the end. You will be more famous than your Newton or your Einstein.'

'But it won't be quite the same,' Albertine says, a little regretfully. 'They did it all by themselves.'

'Perhaps they did.'

'And perhaps they didn't?'

'It is possible, is it not? I am here now, helping you. There could have been others like me, from other civilisations.'

'Yeah,' says Mike, 'but people would have known, wouldn't they? I mean, we know about you.'

'Only because I allow you to know.'

'That's right!' Albertine cries. 'I didn't know about Chocky until Matthew told me. I remember I was very cross with him for daring to suggest that I had been receiving information from an outside source.'

'Exactly. You see, it is all in the mind.'

'Forgive me, Chocky, but we've been wondering,' Su Lin speaks very respectfully, 'how do you make your mind travel? I mean, could we do it too?'

'You already do. You have what you call telepathy. You could communicate now with Matthew, who is thousands of miles away.'

'But that's different, isn't it?'

'In some ways, yes, it is different. You must transmit physical waves from your brains. That is why it will take a little longer for you to reach Matthew in New York than when he was in Sussex. I do not need waves. I can project my whole mind into your world. But the

principles are the same. It works in the same way. You might yet do what I do.'

Albertine gasps. 'You mean, one day, I might be able to project my mind through space to your home?'

'*No*,' says Chocky. '*The individual human mind has not that power.'*

'What if we joined our minds together? All three of us?'

'*I think it would need more than three of you to create such power.'*

'Can we try?' asks Mike, wide-eyed.

'Yes! Let's try now!'

'Please . . .'

'*Be careful, now . . .'*

'Come on,' says Albertine. 'We must all sit facing each other and holding hands.'

They rearrange their chairs. Fingers grasp.

'Now, think of a planet.' Albertine says. She is now breathing very deeply.

'Mars,' says Mike quickly.

'Mars . . .' says Albertine.

'Mars . . .' says Su Lin.

'All together, now. Concentrate.'

All three children now close their eyes. All three breathe deeply and evenly. They begin to frown. Their eyes tighten. Their lips draw back. Sweat breaks from Mike's brow and runs down the sides of his nose. Albertine begins to shake. Only Su Lin remains statuesque and serene, but when at last their concentration snaps and Albertine laughs, 'It's no use!' it is Su Lin who appears to crumple most completely.

'We're not powerful enough, eh?' says Mike.

'*I fear not. The waves that you transmitted will reach Mars, but you will know nothing of it. You have not the strength to transmit a consciousness.'*

'Ah, well, what the heck, Come on. Let's get down to some work.'

'Right, Ladies and Gentlemen,' Meyer's voice booms through the Faculty examination room and buzzes in the walls, 'to work!'

Two hundred small hands rip open envelopes. Two hundred pens are uncapped. Two hundred heads bow low over examination papers.

Soon the bustle makes way for stillness. Soon afterwards the stillness is replaced by sounds familiar to all invigilators: a lot of sighing, head scratching, pen-dropping, teeth-grinding and nervous coughing. Meyer smiles to himself and turns back to his book. Two hundred normal happy children might now be able to resume normal happy lives ...

Several of the children who sat that impromptu exam have assured me that they saw 'this light' floating about the room. Not a bright light, such as David Gore and Matthew, Albertine, Ferris and Wade have reported – just a soft little light: 'Like light reflected from a stream on the bows of a boat.'

'Maybe I'm imagining things,' said George Walford, a thirteen-year old from Stamford, 'but I wouldn't have noticed this light if it had stayed still. It's just that it seemed to be going over each one of us in turn, as though someone were flashing a torch over all of us, checking us out ....'

Paul Barclay sees the light. He too follows it around with his eyes, It bobs slowly all the way along the row in front of him, then down his own row. It rests above his head. He looks up, a little puzzled. The light moves on. Paul looks over to the window, curious. There is no obvious light source. Perhaps someone outside with a mirror.

And then something funny happens. The light returns to Paul. It seems to wrap itself around him, enveloping his head and his shoulders. Suddenly Meyer (who sees no light) observes the boy look up. A range of expressions flickers across his face like fingers across harpstrings: momentary fear, puzzlement, contentment, excitement, joy. And at last, with a broad grin, Paul leans forward. He begins to write.

'Ow!' Su Lin's palm slaps her forehead.

Albertine rocks backward and forward over the keyboard, her face screwed up in a grimace of pain. 'Stop it!' she cries.

'It's not me!' Mike hits the table rapidly with his fist. 'It's somebody new.'

'Yes,' Albertine blinks. 'Chocky's found somebody.'

'He's coming through very strong.'

'Too strong.' Su Lin shakes her head as though to dislodge some insect from her nose. 'It hurts!'

'Hey, man – wherever you are – cool it! For Pete's sake!'

'Can you identify anything about him?' asks Albertine.

'Nope. It's a him. I know that.'

'It's as though he's just discovered his new strength and he's playing with it,' says Su Lin.

'Chocky!' calls Albertine. 'Make him stop!'

Suddenly, Paul laughs. A quick triumphant laugh which slaps at the ceiling and rings in the beams.

The other children look around at him. Some scowl. Some hush him. Laughter is out of place.

'Get back to work,' says Meyer quietly. He stands and steps down from the dais. He goes up to Paul's desk and leans over the back of his chair. His hands rest on the desk. 'Are you all right?' he murmurs in the boy's ear.

'Yes,' Paul says happily. He is a dark, slightly plump boy. His lips are a bare six inches from Meyer's. His breath is warm on his face. 'Yes, sir, I'm fine.'

Meyer's eyes swivel back and forth over the papers on the boy's desk. He frowns. 'How many questions have you done?'

'All of them, sir.'

'All of them? But you only had to choose five.'

'Yes, sir, I know, but I couldn't make up my mind. They all looked interesting.' He grins.

Meyer raises his eyebrows and nods thoughtfully. 'Mind if I take these back to my desk with me?'

'No, sir. What do I do?'

Meyer's lips curl. 'Tell you what. We've got an hour left. Write me something on the subject of cosmic energy.'

Chapter six

'Albertine!' Meyer calls down the cellar stairs. 'Albertine, Su Lin, Mike, come up here. There's someone I want you to meet!'

There is a lot of thumping and giggling from downstairs as he leads Paul into the living room. 'Right,' Meyer says when at last the children stand ranked before him like soldiers at ease. 'Paul, this is my daughter Albertine.'

'Hello,' Albertine nods.

'And Su Lin from Hong Kong,'

'Hi.'

'And Mike. He's from Boston.'

'Boston, Massachusetts,' Mike drawls. 'Hi, Paul.'

'Hi,' Paul grins from the armchair.

Suddenly all three children yelp. Their hands fly to their temples.

'Paul! Stop that,' cries Albertine.

Meyer jumps to his feet. 'What's happening?'

Paul shrugs and shakes his head, bewildered.

'Don't do that, man!' Mike says, then, 'Phew!' And all the children relax and smile once more.

'Sorry.' Paul nervously returns their smiles. 'I didn't know . . .'

'What happened?' Meyer demands. 'I want to know what happened.'

'Don't worry, Daddy. It's OK.'

'You're sure?'

'Yes, honestly, Daddy.'

'All right. I'll leave you to get to know each other.

I've got to make some calls, then we'll go for that walk, all right?'

The room seems to sigh as he leaves. For a moment or two there is silence, then Su Lin sits down opposite Paul and says, 'It was you before, wasn't it?'

'What?' Paul frowns.

'He doesn't know.' Mike perches on the corner of the desk.

Paul shrugs. 'So tell me.' The other children look at one another and nod. 'I mean . . . Hey! I can hear you! I can hear you all! What's happening here?'

'It's called telepathy,' Albertine kneels down at his feet.

'Do you all have it?'

'Yes. Lots of people do in their own ways, but we're lucky. We're special. Ours comes from being in contact with someone called – Chocky.' She speaks the name slowly and deliberately as though to a small child. She is gauging his reactions.

Paul just says, 'Funny sort of name . . .'

'Ah, you don't know about Chocky, do you?'

'No. Who is this Chocky?' An edge of irritation enters his voice.

'Chocky is our friend,' says Su Lin.

Albertine takes Paul's hand. 'Listen,' she says, 'she comes from a distant planet – or rather, her mind does. She's been in contact with you, although you don't know it. That's why you can communicate with us telepathically. She is teaching us some very important things.'

'Like how to talk to each other without speaking, you mean?'

'No, no. That's just a small part of it. That just happens. She is teaching us to use the power of our minds to understand things that nobody else can.'

68

'I still don't get it,' Paul says plaintively. 'The power of your minds?'

'Yup.' Mike stands and saunters over. 'See, very few people know what their minds can achieve. Like – well, we can move things around without touching them, for example.'

'You can?' Paul gapes. 'Wow! How do you do that?'

'By thinking,' Albertine explains in her best maternal tones. 'And to achieve something really big, we join our minds together. It's called a *gestalt*. That's what really matters. When all of us join our minds together, we possess incredible power.'

'Show me?' Paul's grip tightens on Albertine's hand. 'Show me. Please.'

Albertine glances over her shoulder. Again an unspoken conference seems to take place. 'OK.' she turns back to Paul. 'We're going to clear the room as we would if we were having a dance.'

She stands and nods to the others. 'Ready? The settee first, then.'

All three turn to look at the settee. It rolls back towards the wall of its own accord. The back of the settee rests up against the olive green flock on the wall, a good four feet away from where it was just half a minute before.

Paul says, 'Wow!' and laughs.

'Hold on,' Albertine raises a hand, 'we haven't finished yet.'

She and Su Lin walk over to join Mike in the office area at the end of the room. Now they stare at the big Tree of Life rug at the centre.

The corners of the rug flap a couple of times, then the whole thing arises smoothly and rolls itself up. With a cry of 'Hey!' Paul raises his feet just in time.

He puts them down again on bare polished boards. 'This,' he says, 'is weird.'

Mike cackles and clicks his fingers. 'OK, and – music!' He points at the old Bush wireless in the corner. Brahms floods out. 'Not that sort of music!' The tuning knob turns. The machine fizzes and whistles. Some funky jazz-rock stuff, all blazing horns and pounding bass, streams from the big old speaker. 'Whoop!' Mike yells, and he's out on the floor, break-dancing brilliantly. Paul is standing and clapping. Albertine is smiling. Su Lin giggles. Mike spins on his back, then in one smooth movement jerks himself on to his feet and drops in a deadman dive, at that moment the On/Off knob on the wireless turns. The music stops.

'Hey!' Mike complains. Suddenly he looks rather foolish. But no one is looking at him anymore. They are gazing up at a point somewhere above the tall boy.

'Sorry, Mike. That was very good.'

'Chocky!' Albertine cries.

'Chocky . . . ' Paul gasps. 'This is Chocky?'

'That is right, Paul. Welcome to our group.'

'Er . . . thank you.'

'I am very pleased to have found you. You have a very rare, very special mind.'

'I do?'

'Yes, Communication with you is very intense. Together, we shall all achieve great things.'

'Oh, yes.' Paul's smile is uninhibited, ecstatic. 'Oh, yes please, Chocky.'

The door opens. It bangs against the bookcase. 'What the devil was that abysmal row?' Meyer glowers. 'This is meant to be a place of work, not a dance hall, *what* in the Lord's name have you been doing with the furniture? Put it back at once. Albertine, I'm ashamed of you. I do not expect this sort of – frivolity – from my daughter.'

'Yes, Daddy,' she says politely, but there is a lilt of laughter in her voice and she winks up at the tall boy as she crosses the room to roll out the carpet again.

Meyer's temper improves a little when once the living-room is restored to its conventional order. He consents to take all four children on the promised walk along the backs, the banks of the river Cam, from which the loveliest of the colleges can be seen at their best.

Leaning on the balustrade of Trinity Bridge as they pass, is a woman. She is watching them, shielding her eyes from the rays of the sinking sun. She is encased in a smart, severe black chalkstripe suit.

Pru Gibson jots something in her note-book before moving on, just a hundred yards behind them.

'Paul's arrival speeded up our work quite consider-ably,' Albertine wrote (January 2nd from Taraxcon, Provence.) 'He settled in immediately as part of the team. The first suggestion that he made, incidentally, was that instead of keying all the data into the computer, we should simply think it in by our tele-kinetic power. It was a brilliant idea, but the com-puter wasn't up to it. It flashed and popped and puffed out a lot of smoke and came out with its hands up (Mike's description, not mine). So then we had to reconstruct it, and in fact we made quite a lot of improvements to the basic design.

'By Christmas, we were ready to start building the prototype cosmic ray collector. First, of course, we had to select the best shape for it. There were a number of possibilities and Chocky did not know which would work in our atmosphere and gravity. What worked marvellously on her planet might prove a total dud here. We started with the cylinder. The only trouble was that the shopping-list which Chocky gave us contained some very expensive items: Osmium, for example – one of the platinum metals, but the only element of sufficient density for our purposes. Professor Wade began to fuss. We were working fast, but the grant was running out just as quickly. Anyhow, we bought all the necessary constituents; Professor Wade had a cylinder of the right proportions constructed in her workshop and at last the day came for the great unveiling – January 27th . . .'

The cylinder is squat and shiny – perhaps three feet long and eighteen inches in diameter. At the moment, it lies in two semi-cylindrical parts on the formica-topped table. In absolute silence, Mike, Paul, Su Lin and Albertine connect wires with soldering irons. Each seems to know exactly what the other is doing. It is as though they have done it all before. Not a movement is wasted.

Upstairs, Meyer and Jean Wade sit waiting. They have emptied a pot of coffee and have strolled in silence around the snow-dusted garden since Wade delivered the cylinder shell at eleven this morning. Now it is three twenty-one, twenty-two. Occasionally Meyer stands and walks to the window, only to return to his chair a minute or two later. Wade's head has fallen forward. Her eyelids have drooped, snapped open, drooped, snapped open. Her breathing is heavy and even. The gas fire roars.

*

The children are weary now too. It is twelve minutes past four. At last, the soldering irons are laid on the table. Still without a word, they exchange a thought. Albertine nods, smiles reassuringly and goes upstairs.

'We're ready,' she announces, and Wade awakes with a start.

When she returns with the adults, Su Lin and Paul are standing at opposite corners of the table. Mike holds the final piece of metal in one hand, a pair of tweezers in the other.

Wade and Meyer shuffle sideways to the far end of the room. Albertine takes her place at Mike side.

'All right,' says Meyer. 'We're ready.'

'Isn't this *exciting*?' Wade beams.

'It could be one of the truly great moments in scientific history.'

'OK,' Mike's shrill voice breaks through the solemn mood. 'Here we go, then . . .'

He bends over the semi-cylinder and carefully puts the last piece in place. The tweezers gleam.

'Right,' says Albertine, 'now we put the two halves together . . .'

She and Mike pick up one half of the cylinder. Paul picks up the other. Very carefully, they push them together. There is a click. You can't even see the join. It is a perfect cylinder, standing on its end.

'. . . and . . .'

And nothing. They wait for a full ten seconds. Nothing happens. Ten seconds more. Still, nothing. The children exchange glances. Meyer does not look at Wade.

'Um,' he says at last, 'what exactly . . .?'

'Nothing,' says Su Lin. 'It doesn't work, that's all.'

'Oh *dear*,' Wade moans. 'Oh dear, oh dear, oh dear . . .'

*

'That was bad enough,' wrote Albertine, 'And we were all pretty depressed. Chocky, of course, was full of confidence and good cheer. Chocky doesn't have to worry about tedious things like bank balances. Paul in particular seemed down. Again and again I heard him sobbing in bed at night but he shut off his mind so that we couldn't find out what was wrong. He told me in the end. I went into his bedroom and he told me. Basically, it was just homesickness. He hadn't seen his mother for many years and, like me, he still missed her. Like me, he had lived with his father since they split up, and now he felt that he could not go and see him either.

'I told him that of course he must go home whenever he wanted to. He seemed rather surprised, almost as though he had thought that he would never see his father again. The next day he arranged to return home for a weekend two weeks later . . .

'Meanwhile, we got to work on the second shape – this time, a sphere. Having done the innards once before, we were much quicker this time. We had everything ready but the shells by the time that Paul left. It was up to Professor Wade to cast the shells, so our work was done. We needed a break too, so we took an afternoon off to go tobogganing up in the hills . . .'

'Professor Draycott.' Meyer is reserved but polite. 'How good of you to call. Do come in.'

Draycott's hat drips snow. He snuffles and sighs and steams. 'God-forsaken weather,' he fumes. 'Hate it.' He hands Meyer his sodden coat.

'Well, come on into the warm and sit down.' Meyer leads him into the living-room. 'Can I get you anything? Tea? Coffee?'

'No, thank you, Meyer. This is not a social call.'

'Oh, well.' Meyer sits at his desk.' I'm afraid the children are out at the moment.'

'Never mind,' Draycott snaps. 'I'd like to know how they're getting on.'

'They seem to be getting on fine, thank you,' says Meyer evenly. 'They're working very hard.'

'But not on the day that I chance to call, hmm? You must understand, Meyer, that I am under increasing pressure to justify this extraordinary project. Poor Dr Liddle, for example, has been doing excellent work, really excellent, and she has some startling findings to show for it. She needs a grant badly. Now, have your little researchers anything to show for their labours?'

'Well,' something tugs at the corner of Meyer's mouth, 'it is early days yet, Professor.'

'I understood that they'd already built something?'

'Er, yes,' Meyer nods, 'but it wasn't successful.'

'Ha!' Draycott barks. Meyer jumps. 'May I see this expensive failure?'

Meyer raises an eyebrow. 'Why?'

'Because I'm interested, Meyer, that's why. As a member of the committee responsible for giving the grant, you understand. Surely, I have the right . . .'

'Oh, yes, yes.' Meyer stands. 'Of course. It's in the lab. Come this way . . .'

Albertine is rolling off her toboggan in the snow, throwing snowballs, playing silly games. Just for a few hours, university politics and cosmic rays are forgotten. Her usually pale cheeks are red and wet. Her hair is matted with snow.

They only have one toboggan between the three of them – a plastic skidpan which is far better suited to this soft snow than the sleds with steel runners which other children have brought out on to the hill. Albertine has just come down, Mike clinging on to her shoulders. Inevitably, at the bottom, the toboggan turned over, sending both children tumbling. Now Mike pulls the skidpan back up the hill to where Su Lin awaits them.

'Phew, I'm whacked!' At the top, he slumps down and throws himself back on to the snow.

Su Lin catches Albertine's eye. Albertine nods. They don't need particularly highly-developed telepathic powers for this one. As Mike lies back and squints up at the sun, they bend and fill their arms with snow. Albertine nods to Su Lin.

'You ... you pigs!' Mike sits up spluttering and giggling and spitting out snow. 'I'll get you for this!' And he's up and running and flinging snowballs at the girls as fast as he can gather them.

When at last the battle is over and all three are flat on their backs and panting, their breath bouncing back over their brows, it is Su Lin who sits up and says, 'Hey! Look! The sleigh!'

She points. Albertine and Mike stand and shake snow from their clothes. Their sleigh has got impatient and set off on its own.

'Oh, no!' Mike groans. 'I'm not going all the way down there again!'

Again that exchange of glances. 'Shall we?' says Mike.

'Should we?' says Su Lin.

'Let's.'

They join hands.

Two innocent children and their father are just trudging up the hill to start their afternoon's sport. 'Daddy, look!' One little girl grasps his hand and tugs.

'It's magic!' gasps her elder sister.

'Nonsense,' says her father, who prides himself upon his rationalism, 'um . . . it's . . . there's some sort of string . . . it's . . . Good Lord . . . It's an optical illusion of some sorts, a joke.' And as the toboggan reaches Albertine's waiting hand at the top of the hill, he shakes his head and stumbles. 'Er, look,' he says. 'I don't think this is much of a hill, do you? Maybe we should try somewhere else . . .'

'Oh, Daddy!'

'Don't argue. Gwen. Come along. Hurry up!'

'This,' Meyer lifts down the cylinder, 'was the prototype.'

'Hmm.' Draycott eyes it suspiciously. 'And what precisely was it supposed to do – if it had worked, that is?'

'It was meant to collect cosmic rays, and muons.'

'Was it indeed?' Draycott sneers. 'And how exactly was it meant to do that?'

'I – I'm not actually certain,' Meyer admits.

'I see,' Draycott muses briskly. He bends and pokes at the prototype's innards with a pencil. 'Tell me, if it had been successful, what would they have done with the cosmic rays and muons?'

'Well, er . . .'

'How would they have applied them? And to what?'

'I have no idea. Chocky hasn't told us that yet,' Meyer admits miserably.

Draycott straightens. His eyebrows shoot up. He glances at his watch. 'Chocky. Hmm. Thank you, Mr Meyer. All I wanted to know. I'll see myself out.'

Chapter seven

Paul is back, refreshed and happy. The twin hemi-
spheres have been cast. All that now remains is to
place the mechanism inside them. A few fine
adjustments – a matter of an hour or two, and this
shape too will be ready for trial. But the pressure is
on now. They know that. There is little money left,
and Draycott's visit makes it clear that they have
powerful enemies.

This evening, Meyer has been summoned to a
Faculty Grants Committee meeting. He knows that
the news that he will bring back will not be good.
The only question is how bad it will be.

Meanwhile, the children can do nothing but work
and forget their worries.

'This time it's got to work.' Albertine raises her
head from the hemisphere on which she is working.
'Understood, Chocky?'

'Yes. I understand, Albertine.'

'Don't worry,' Paul sniffs. 'This one will work.'

'Howd'ye know that?' asks Mike.

'I just know,' Paul shrugs. 'Come on. Let's get on
with it.'

It is Meyer now who sits on the hard chair and
faces the professional inquisition. No one, however,
seems to wish to quiz him. He is there as a witness,
no more.

'I admit,' says Wade, 'that as *yet* there are no results.'

'Well, what do you expect?' Ferris shrugs.

'I expect some sort of positive progress for the amount of money they've had,' says Draycott. 'To date I can see proof of neither theoretical nor practical advance.'

'Yes, but I understood from the outset that there were several possible designs,' Ferris soothes. 'They could not be sure which was the best until they'd made and tested them . . .'

'My understanding *exactly*,' Wade nods.

'I'm not talking about which one is best,' Draycott hums, 'I'm talking about it not doing anything. I inspected their first model, and I could see no indication of any scientific principles whatsoever. If you ask me, they're simply trying to produce yet another conjuring trick.'

'Oh, that's hardly fair!' Meyer breaks in.

'And it is hardly fair on other, reputable scientists – like Dr Liddle, for example – that they cannot continue with research of proven academic worth because these – these *children* – are given the funds they need. I propose – I *insist*, Mr Meyer – that we should here and now give your infants a deadline to show us something positive. I do not ask much – just some proof that the whole thing is not a wild goose chase. And if they can't, we cut off the funds.'

'And how long do you propose that we should give them?' asks Ferris in a voice like muffled drums.

Meyer places his forefinger over one eye, his thumb over the other, and an involuntary groan forces its way up from somewhere deep within him.

'OK,' Mike holds up his gleaming hemisphere. 'Ready your side?'

'Yup. All finished,' says Albertine. 'Here goes.'

Feet clatter on the stairs. Meyer rushes into the

79

cellar. Albertine turns to him, her finger to her lips, 'Sh! We're almost there!'

'I've got to talk to you all,' Meyer whispers urgently.

'Not now, Daddy. Wait! Watch!'

Su Lin lays one hemisphere on the table with its inner workings turned upwards. Very, very cautiously, Albertine and Mike lower the other on to it. Again there is a click. Again the line at the join vanishes. They stand back to watch it, a perfect shining sphere.

Nothing happens.

'Oh, dear . . .' Meyer starts.

'Shhh!' Albertine is imperious. 'Look. Watch!'

'Yes,' says Mike quietly.

'Yes,' says Paul.

'Yes,' says Su Lin.

'It's happening!' Meyer gasps. 'It's happening!'

For a low throbbing sound emerges from the sphere. It begins to glow with an eery orange light. With each throb, the light grows stronger and brighter until there is one continuous humming sound and the light suffuses the whole cellar.

Mike whoops. Su Lin slumps down and sobs. Albertine throws her arms around her father. Paul just stands there, his arms hanging limp at his sides, that ecstatic slow smile once more on his face. 'We did it,' he says softly. 'We did it, we did it, we *did* it!'

Meyer unlocks Albertine's arms from round his neck. 'Now, now,' he says gruffly. 'Well done. Very.' He fishes out a handkerchief and dabs at his cheeks, or maybe at his eyes. 'I came back . . . I came back to tell you that they've given us just one week. If this hadn't worked . . .' he shrugs.

'Oh, don't, Daddy!' Albertine shudders. 'Look! Ring them now!'

'Yes. Yes, I will.' He strides over to the telephone. 'Well done, Su Lin, Paul, Mike,' he nods to each of them as he dials. 'First-rate. Hello? Hello, Professor Ferris? You will be gratified to hear that we've done it. The children have succeeded . . . Yes. Yes. I have it in front of me right now and it's glowing with received energy. It's filling the room with it. Cosmic energy . . . Any time you like, Professor . . . Of course, yes, you must bring them along too. I can't wait to see Draycott's face . . . Yes, nine o'clock tomorrow will be fine. Goodbye.' He turns to face the line of eager and excited young faces. 'They're coming over at nine in the morning,' he says. 'Professor Ferris sends his congratulations.'

'Great.'

'Um . . .' Meyer is at a loss, 'I think probably it's time for bed now, don't you?'

'S'pose so,' Mike shrugs.

'Yes.'

'OK.' Albertine gazes rather wistfully at the sphere.

'Tomorrow we'll think what we should do to celebrate,' he says apologetically.

As soon as the children have trooped from the room, Meyer approaches the glowing sphere. He holds out a tentative hand. It is not even warm. Very carefully, he cups his hands beneath it and picks it up. He lays it in the open wall cupboard and gazes at it for a full minute before closing the door on it. He pockets the key and dragging his feet, trudges back up the stairs.

The living-room lights and the hall lights are extinguished. The bathroom is briefly lit before each of the upstairs squares is blanked out, one by one. The watcher out on the street looks at an illuminated watchface, then back at the darkened house. Only, it is not quite dark. From the grid in the pavement a flush of soft orange light flows over the pavement and creeps up the brick walls. The watcher steps back into the shadows. There is nothing to do now but wait.

'Do come in, gentlemen, Professor Wade,' Albertine holds open the door with a touch of smugness. 'If you'd come this way. The energy-collector is in the laboratory . . .'

She leads them down into the cellar. Meyer and the other children stand waiting about the table. With eight people crammed in there, the laboratory seems suddenly small. 'If you'd all like to stand there, please.' Albertine lines up the three professors along one end of the table. 'Thank you.'

'Isn't it *thrilling*?' Wade gushes. 'To think, we are going to be the very first people ever to see . . .'

'Oh, get on with it,' Draycott grunts. 'For goodness' sake!'

'Don't be such a churl, Draycott,' Ferris says quietly.

'Ready?' Albertine asks. 'Right.' She reaches for the doorknob and flings open the cupboard doors. Because they open outwards she cannot see what lies inside. All that she can see are the faces of her friends. Mike's jaw drops. Su Lin's whole face seems to crumple. Paul gasps and looks to Meyer for enlightenment. 'What . . .' says Albertine and something twists inside her like plastic in the fire. She peers round the door.

The cupboard is empty.

'But . . .' her lower lip trembles, 'Daddy . . .?'

'I don't know!' Meyer shakes his head. 'I don't know.'

'It's gone!'

Su Lin slumps down on to her knees. She rests her forehead on her arm and sobs uncontrollably, Mike rests his left hand on her head. His right clenches into a trembling fist.

'I don't understand,' bleats Ferris.

'What is this?' Draycott demands. 'What are you trying to do?'

'It was *here*!' Albertine quavers. 'I . . .'

'I put it in this cupboard myself, last night.' Meyer reaches over and runs his hand along the shelf as though to discover a false bottom. 'I put it in this cupboard myself. I put it . . .'

'You expect us to believe that?'

'It's true!' the children cry in unison. 'It's true!'

'Oh, dear,' Wade smooths down her skirt. 'How very, very unfortunate.'

'I don't know what sort of childish game you think you're playing,' Draycott spits out the words in foul-tasting chunks, 'but I am tired of having my time – and the university's money, wasted. Ferris, Wade, I suggest we meet later to organise where this grant may more profitably be awarded. Good morning.'

Wade and Ferris leave soon afterwards. They seem able to say little more than 'oh, dear'.

Each of the children reacts differently. Paul seems to shrink inside himself. He just sits in the garden and stares at the wall. Su Lin goes down to the river and cries to the ducks. Mike kicks a lot of things – walls, car-tyres, trees, in a long walk out towards Grant-chester. Albertine just runs up to bed and sobs her heart out.

She has been there for just a minute when she knows that Chocky is there above her head. She does not look up. She just continues to chew on her sheet and to sob while her knees arise to her chest and straighten again and again.

'Do not cry, Albertine.'

'Oh, Chocky. Chocky. I'm sorry.'

'It was not your fault.'

'But—but what happened?' she wails. 'It couldn't just disappear into thin air.'

'No. Someone must have taken it.'

'But who? Who would do such a thing?'

'I do not know, but never mind. Now that we have found the right shape, and proved that it works on your planet, we can easily make another one.'

'No, Chocky, no! You don't understand!' She pounds at the damp pillow. 'Each new model costs thousands of pounds. We've used up all our money! Unless we get the next part of our grant, we can't buy any more materials. Mike and Su Lin and Paul will all have to go home. It's over, Chocky. The whole thing. It's over!'

Tea in the kitchen is a cheerless affair. To compound the gloom, it is raining now, and the best that Albertine and her father have been able to muster is baked beans on toast. No one but Mike wants to eat. They just sit glumly at the table, listening to the rain as it batters the windows. They cannot help recalling last night's elation and Meyer's words. 'Tomorrow we'll think what we can do to celebrate.'

'At least you'll be able to keep in touch with one another,' Meyer sighs at last.

'Yeah,' says Mike, 'but my parents wouldn't let me come again even if we got the money.'

'Oh!' Su Lin says savagely. Everyone turns to look at her, but she has nothing more to say.

'If only we could find it,' Paul blinks swollen eyes, 'at least we could take it to someone else and get them to give us the money. Oh, I don't know.' He throws his head back and studies the ceiling. He has to sniff several times.

The doorbell rings. No one moves. It rings again, a longer, louder ring this time. 'I'll get rid of them,' Albertine throws down her napkin.

More rain spatters the window. They can hear Albertine's voice from the hall, but they cannot distinguish her words.

'Oh,' Su Lin's voice aches, 'I could kill . . .'

Mike pours more tea. 'Easy,' he says. 'Easy.'

Albertine slouches back into the room. 'This lady insists on talking to us. All of us.' She throws herself down into her chair.

This lady steps briskly into the doorway and stands there pulling off her gloves. She wears shiny black court shoes, smooth black stockings and a stern, smart maroon suit. Meyer thinks that he has seen her before. None of the others knows her.

'Hello,' she says. 'My name is Mrs Gibson. Pru Gibson.'

Only Meyer starts to get up. The children just stare sullenly at their congealing food. She does not seem to notice. She walks blithely over to Meyer and hands him her card.

'Prudence Gibson,' Meyer reads, 'Ministry of Science.'

'Oh,' says Albertine, as though this explains everything. 'So you work for the government.'

'That's right, Albertine,' she says brightly, 'the British Government. May I sit down?'

'Of course.' Meyer shakes himself. 'Forgive me. I'm sorry.'

He pulls out the remaining kitchen chair. She sits. Very neatly, as she seems to do everything, she places the black patent handbag at her feet.

'Now!' she says in a cheery, voice, 'you must be Su Lin. How do you do? Mike, Paul, I'm delighted to meet you. Sorry to disturb your meal. Not that you seem to have much appetite. Pity. I do like to see children doing themselves well . . .'

Each child in turn has sat up as she names them. Now they frown curiously at one another.

'How do you know our names?' Albertine asks.

'Oh, but the government is very interested in all of you, Albertine! And in your work.'

Albertine raises her shoulders and lowers her head. 'We have no work,' she speaks into her teacup.

'I'm afraid you've come at a bad time, Mrs Gibson,' Meyer explains. 'We've just heard that our project is to be cancelled.'

'Yes,' she says calmly, 'I know.'

'But *how*?' Albertine asks, exasperated.

'As I said, the government is very interested in you.'

'In our research into gifted children?'

'Of course, Mr Meyer.' Mrs Gibson flashes a quick, knowing smile. 'And in your research into cosmic energy.'

Now all the children are wide awake. They sit forward frowning. Their mouths are taut, thin lines.

'Don't worry, don't worry!' she sings. 'I've been sent to look after you! We are well aware that there have been one or two threats from unscrupulous business interests in the past, hmm, Albertine? And we don't want that sort of thing happening again, now do we?'

86

'We certainly do not,' says Meyer drily.

'Good! Good! So, if you'll just put yourselves into my hands, everything will be just ticketyboo, as my old nanny would say. And you can all stop looking so gloomy. My ministry is more than happy to give you all the money you need to continue with your work, so I suggest that we throw away all this disgusting food, and I'll have a look in the 'fridge and . . .'

She manages to get just this far before her words sink in and suddenly her voice is drowned by whoops and cheers and thumping on the table as all four children leap to their feet and shake hands and embrace (Mike even hugs a startled Mrs Gibson) and a giant clap of thunder shakes the walls and windows and twists grumbling away through the charred paper clouds above Cambridge.

Chapter eight

'It didn't take long after that to construct the new energy collector,' wrote Albertine. 'We were practised. We knew where everything should go, and we weren't under constant pressure. It's much easier to work fast if there isn't someone looking over your shoulder and telling you to hurry all the time.

'By now, too, we had come fully to understand why we were doing what we were doing. As Chocky had told us it would, everything was becoming obvious. Poor Daddy, of course, had not had Chocky to help him. He kept asking where the generator was – things like that. Natural enough questions if you're used to thinking in terms of electricity, but totally meaningless in terms of cosmic rays.

'Basically, cosmic energy has been around since first stars began to condense. Chocky says that supernova explosions, just like the one which transmuted helium into the magnesium, aluminium, silicon, iron, lead, uranium and so on of our earth, also created – and still create in every galaxy – the limitless cosmic rays which pass through us all the time. By collecting these omnipresent rays (I say omnipresent, but I suppose they would not be present where there was no interstellar gas(?)) our sphere becomes at once a generator and a battery. It is so difficult to explain. You really have to work with Chocky to understand it all. We just do not as yet have the language for it – even in mathematics.

'Anyhow, we constructed a new sphere, and this

time, we decided to keep it to ourselves. We just got on with the next stage, the building of the anti-gravitational screens.

'Only one thing disturbed our cottage industry at that time. As I've told you before, Paul sleeps in the room next to mine. The very night on which we completed the sphere and once more it was glowing away down in the lab, I was unable to sleep. You know how it can be when you've been working very hard? You are so tired that you cannot sleep. The mind will not switch off, even though the body aches.

'It must have been soon after one o'clock when I heard a rustling and the creak of the floorboards as Paul got out of bed. I thought that he must just be going to the loo, but a moment later I heard him padding down the stairs. Everything creaked in that house. Then came the quiet slap of his bare soles on the hall tiles, the click of the cellar door latch.

'I climbed out of bed as quietly as I could. I slipped on my dressing-gown and my slippers. I went down after him.

'Down in the dark hallway, it suddenly struck me that it might not after all have been Paul that I had heard. Perhaps our visitor had returned. The thought scared me, but my fear for the sphere and my anger at whoever had stolen it were far greater than my fear for myself.

'The door at the top of the cellar stairs was still open, so I made no sound as I tiptoed down towards the soft orange light.

'Whoever it was had the cupboard doors open. I could therefore see nothing but the shadows cast on the stone wall by the glowing sphere and silhouetted legs beneath the doors. I fumbled for the light switch. The strip lights flashed four times before at last they came on. The person at the cupboard did not move. When at last the white light filled the room, I recognised at once the blue and white-striped pyjama legs.

'"Paul!" I called. I walked down into the room. Paul did not turn. He was just standing there, holding the sphere in both hands like a priest with a chalice. "Paul!" I reached out and touched him. "Paul!"

'He sort of shuddered. He put down the sphere and rubbed his eyes. He turned and blinked at me rather foolishly. "What?" he said. "Where? What's happening?"

'"What are you doing?" I asked.

'He said, "I don't know. I'm sorry. What ...?" and shook his head.

'Then of course Daddy came down, and Mrs Gibson, and neither of them would quite look straight at poor Paul, though everyone was being terribly nice. Sleepwalking, you know. Too much hard work. Go to bed. Don't worry about it. But I knew what they were thinking and so did Paul, and when at last we'd had a cup of Horlicks and returned to bed, I'm afraid that I found myself thinking it too. Had Paul really been sleepwalking, or had he perhaps taken a similar night walk four weeks before when the collector vanished?

'Anyhow, aside from this little bit of excitement, all was peace and industry, and soon we had finished the first of the anti-gravitational screens . . .'

The anti-gravitational screen is a large triangular structure made of a black material which resembles obsidian. It is lighter than obsidian, however, and the children can handle it with ease. They have painstakingly covered its surface with smaller reflective pyramids and, for once, the usually spick and span laboratory looks like a motor mechanic's workshop.

There are bits and pieces scattered everywhere.

What did Dr Liddle have to say about this period? It is important both to the tale and of course, in the history of science. Everyone has read about her findings in the newspapers and the science journals, but in an interview with me she revealed for the first time how she came to make her discovery.

'I had been studying for some time a new binary star on the outer edge of the Andromeda extragalactic nebula which, as you know, is very similar to our own galaxy and only about 700,000 light years away. I had been taking readings from it for nine months, if you include the ten days or so during which the Meyer girl changed the program. The interesting thing about these read-outs was that they were remarkably consistent in character. They appeared, if it is not a foolish thing to say – to be rhythmical in nature. I did not understand this, and could not conceive – foolishly as it now seems to me – a possible explanation.

'Then one day, feeling just a little frustrated by the unchanging nature of the signals that I received from my binary, I happened to take a look at what young Albertine had been doing. The co-ordinates were all in the computer's memory, with the time code. I called them up, then aligned the telescope on them.

'And what I found was impossible. The read-outs from her alignment were identical with those from my binary. They too were rhythmical and they had precisely the same rhythm. I checked and I double-checked. After all, any two stars are as different as any two sets of fingerprints, yet even after a month, there was not a single difference between the one set of readings and the other.

'I reported this to Wilfrid Draycott. I thought that he'd just laugh at me. I had even begun to think that I must be going mad. But then he told me something that he hadn't dared to tell me before – again, because he was afraid that I would laugh. He told me that young Meyer had claimed to have found an intelligent life form from outer space. She said that she had received signals, not from the planet that she sought, but from a colony of that planet. Now, the regularity of these read-outs argued that an intelligent creature was sending them. The fact that both sets of signals were identical argued that they were sent by the same or by related intelligences. Albertine's explanation was the *only* logical explanation. Then Draycott told me about this Chocky creature. I could have killed him for not telling me before . . .'

At last the final pyramid has been fixed to the triangle.

The children step back and eye their handiwork with pride. They have not spoken aloud for two hours or more, but now Paul looks up at the ceiling and asks, 'Can we test it now?'

'Yes,' says Chocky, *'but first you must activate the screen.'*

'How do we do that?' asks Su Lin.

'With the collector, of course,' says Albertine.

'Oh, yes, of course.'

Mike fetches the glowing ball from the cupboard. 'Where do we put it, Chocky?'

'At one vertex of the triangle.'

'Like this?' He bends down and places the collector at the bottom right-hand corner of the screen. It lodges there between two of the small pyramids as though held by a magnet. Brilliant light ripples across the surfaces of the pyramids. It makes the whole triangle appear to move. Aside from the steady low hum of the sphere, there is no sound.

'Is that it?' Albertine asks quietly.

'Why don't you find out for yourselves?'

Albertine nods. She looks around the table. The remains of their lunch lie scattered on a tray. She reaches for an orange. In three slow strides she is standing by the triangle. Very tentatively, she holds the orange out above the glittering surface. Her fingers open. She lowers her hand. As she does so, a little gasped 'oh!' escapes from her parted lips. She draws her hand back and wipes it nervously on her jeans. The orange floats unmoving five feet above the triangle.

There is a moment's respectful silence, then Mike punches Paul's shoulder and yells, 'Right!' and Su Lin shrills, 'Wheee!' and suddenly the serious young scientists are children again, giggling and dancing and slapping one another's backs.

'Wait!' calls Su Lin, 'I've got an idea . . .' Smiling broadly, she picks up the big glass water jug.

'What are you up to?' Albertine grins. 'Oh, yes!'

Su Lin giggles. She stands tiptoe and reaches up above the orange. She tilts the jug, then turns it on its end. The water remains at the bottom – or rather the top of the jug.

There is more laughter, more excitement, as Su Lin steps back, leaving the jug floating there. Mike steps forward. He holds up his hands and thinks a question. Three pairs of eyes twinkle and smile at him.

'What are we waiting for?' Albertine shrugs.

She steps forward and raises first one foot, then the other. She sinks a couple of inches, then bobs up again as though in water. She looks down at her feet.

She giggles. She is suspended eighteen inches above the ground. She starts to sing a tuneless song. She pirouettes. 'Come on!' she sings. 'It's lovely!'

Mike is the first to join her. He puts both feet together and makes a standing jump. He sinks to within an inch of the triangle but is instantly borne up still higher than Albertine.

Su Lin takes Mike's hand and steps up. Her skirt flies up. She giggles, pulls it down again, then abandons modesty and stands upright to join hands with the others.

Only Paul remains a wallflower. He gapes up at them, bemused, until Mike calls, 'Come on in, the water's lovely. Lot more fun than sleepwalking!' Then Paul gives his characteristic sniff and steps forward to join them. As he stretches up a hand to Albertine, the door swings inward.

'Right, everybody,' Meyer drones, 'break time! I ...' He steps around the corner. He stops. Mrs Gibson, following close behind, bumps into him and yelps. A strange little burbling sound dribbles from Meyer's lips. He tries to point, but his hands are full of tea-tray. The tray tilts. The teapot topples first, then the milk-bottle falls to the floor with a crash. Thanks to some skilful juggling, he saves all but one cup. As milk and tea spread and merge on the stone flags, he tries to lay the tray down on the table, but he can concentrate on nothing but the children. Su Lin is doubled up with laughter. Mike is actually lying now on his bed of air, kicking his heels and hooting. 'But ...' gasps Meyer, 'but ... but ...'

'Good Lord,' says Mrs Gibson. 'Heavens above. I mean, really!'

*

'That was amazing,' Mrs Gibson shakes her head. 'Absolutely phenomenal.'

The china had been swept up, the tea and milk mopped. Two chickens are in the oven. Meyer and Gibson both have glasses of sherry. Su Lin and Mike play duets on the piano.

'Quite astonishing,' Meyer nods. 'I never understood that it would be like that.'

'I know,' Albertine laughs. 'You should have seen your face!'

'Is there any limit to the weight that this thing would support?' Mrs Gibson asks casually.

'Theoretically, no,' says Albertine, 'provided that the object or objects remain within the vertical plane immediately above the triangle.'

'Extraordinary,' she muses. 'Imagine what would happen if you were to incorporate this into the launch pad of a rocket or a miss . . .' she stops herself. 'I mean, there'd be no further need for huge motors and – and things.'

'But you say this is just the beginning, Albertine?' Meyer sips his sherry.

'Mmm. Yes. That triangle is just one side of a pyramid. And don't forget, this is just the first model.'

'One hardly dares to contemplate what comes next,' Meyer smiles. 'You've left me far behind. By the way, where's Paul got to?'

'He said he had a bit of a headache,' Su Lin calls over the top of the piano. 'Wanted to lie down for a while.'

'Oh, well, it's nearly supper time. He must have been up there for two hours or so. Why doesn't one of you go and wake him up?'

'I'll go, Daddy.'

But two minutes later, Albertine is back with a worried expression on her face. 'He's not there,' she announces. 'I can't find him anywhere.'

Mrs Gibson springs to her feet. 'The sphere!'

'It's all right,' Albertine shakes her head, 'I checked. Everything's where it should be. Anyhow, you've got that all wrong. Paul wouldn't do a thing like that.'

'No,' Mrs Gibson relaxes. 'Well. I'm sure you're right, dear, but where on earth has he got to?'

'I have no idea.'

'Su Lin? Mike?'

'Nope.'

Su Lin shakes her head.

'But – I thought that you could all read one another's minds?'

'Yes, but we can't tell what any of the others is thinking unless they want us to,' Albertine explains patiently, 'unless they're actually sending messages.'

'Ah,' Mrs Gibson pounces on this with interest. 'So you can't just tune in to one another, as it were?'

'Oh, no,' says Su Lin, 'that would be horrid.'

'Yes. Yes, I suppose it would. But you can call each other up if you want to?'

'Yes.'

'So why can't you just call Paul and ask him where he is?'

'I've tried,' sighs Albertine. 'He doesn't answer.'

'Still,' Meyer consoles, 'I don't think he can have come to much harm. If he'd been in any danger, he'd have called for help and you'd have heard him.'

'Yes. I think he's all right,' says Albertine. 'Still, I wish I knew what was worrying him. Perhaps he's homesick again.'

'Perhaps,' Mrs Gibson says stiffly, 'but he still

shouldn't just go off like this without telling anyone where he is going. It's most inconsiderate. Well, dinner won't wait for him . . .'

Albertine is up and out of her chair as soon as she hears the click of the front door.

'Paul!' she puts her arm around his neck. 'Where have you been? Why didn't you answer when I called you? We were worried about you.' She feels a little movement of the shoulders beneath her arm, but Paul says nothing.

Together like that, they enter the kitchen. 'He's back,' Albertine says simply. 'Sit down, Paul.' She kneels to take his covered plate from the oven.

'Are you all right?' Meyer asks as Paul sits at his left hand.

'Yes, of course. I needed some fresh air, that's all. I wanted to be on my own for a bit – thanks, Albertine – so I went for a walk.'

'Well, please don't do it again,' says Mrs Gibson briskly. 'Not without telling someone where you are. Right?'

'I'm sorry,' Paul shrugs. He shovels chicken and roast potatoes into his mouth.

'For all we know, anything could have happened to you. I want you to remember this – all of you. You're all very important. You must be on your guard at all times.'

'Oh, you don't have to worry about us, Mrs Gibson.' Mike chews noisily. 'We can look after ourselves.'

'Yes,' says Albertine. 'When we join our minds together, we can stop anybody.'

'Is that so?' Mrs Gibson's eyebrows rise.

'It is indeed, Mrs Gibson,' Meyer confirms. 'I've seen it.'

'Oh,' Mrs Gibson frowns. She stabs with her fork at the last potato on her plate. It skitters off on to the table. 'Well. I didn't know that,' she says.

Chapter nine

'Three more times in the course of the next few weeks I noticed that Paul had vanished. He was never away for more than two or three hours at a time, but on his return he seemed more preoccupied than ever, and he shut off his mind from us, as though afraid that we might catch him unawares. I did not talk to anyone about it, but I was worried.

'You know how it is when someone in a school or something has been stealing? Even the innocent become suspicious and aware that they too are under suspicion. Tension and guilt are everywhere. The whole community suffers. It was a bit like that with Paul. I *knew* that he had nothing to do with the disappearance of our original collector. I knew it, but I wasn't quite sure, which isn't rational, I know, but it does make sense. We all felt like that, but none of us was saying anything. There is nothing worse than a "something we don't mention" for making a group of people suspicious and snappy.

'I vowed that I would try to follow Paul next time he went off on one of his mysterious walks. Please don't make me out to be some sort of spy when you write the book. It was for the good of the whole group, the good of the project. I even thought at the time that it was for Paul's good. Something attracted him or dominated him, and it wasn't making him any happier.

'Meanwhile, of course, there was the rest of the pyramid to construct. It is a simple enough process in itself, but the optimum efficacy of the collector depends upon precision, and that sort of precision costs time. It would have been boring if the end result was not so exciting. I cannot tell you how much we spoke to one another as we worked, because memory finds it difficult to distinguish between thoughts spoken and unspoken. My guess is that, for three weeks or so, we spent most of the day in total silence.

'Oh, you may wonder why I couldn't get Chocky to check out on Paul's thoughts and actions. But, you see, even Chocky cannot penetrate a mind which has shut itself off. Chocky – like God, I suppose – could have picked Paul up and thrown him in the river or whisked him up into orbit, but she battles in vain against the wilful loneliness of humans once the drawbridges are up. She was worried too . . .'

The children are in the lab, working in silence now. They have three faces of the pyramid in position above the square base. Albertine, Su Lin and Paul are at the table. They are busy fitting the smaller pyramids to the last face. Only Mike is actually by the pyramid itself. He is once more at work with the soldering iron.

Each of the equilateral triangles has sides six feet long (Chocky prefers feet and inches. She says that they are illogical but that a decimal system whose basic unit is totally arbitrary is downright stupid.) Pythagoras informs me (when once I have spent two minutes drawing diagrams in the margin) that the whole structure is therefore five feet high.

Mike is on his back. He wriggles backward so that his head is just inside the pyramid, and he reaches up to solder a join.

A few moments pass.

'Hey, you guys,' Mike pulls himself out and sits up. 'What's the matter with you? Pay attention, will you?'

'What?'

'Well, you might answer me when I ask you a question.'

'When?'

'When I was inside there,' Mike squeaks. He points over his shoulder. 'I asked what time you reckoned we'd be finished?'

'I didn't hear you,' Albertine shakes her head.

'Nor I.'

'Nope.'

'Yeah, well, I didn't speak. I *thought*.'

'No, you didn't,' says Paul.

'Man, I know when I think.' Mike is bullish. 'I thought you guys a question!'

'And we didn't hear it ...' Su Lin is pensive. 'Perhaps – perhaps it's got something to do with the pyramid. Try it again, Mike.'

Mike shrugs and lies back. The three others stand stock still. They watch his headless form intently. Albertine frowns. 'No, Mike!' she calls. Mike sits up again. 'Nothing?' The children shake their heads. 'This is *weird*.'

'Hang on,' says Su Lin. 'Let me try.'

Mike stands as Su Lin crosses the room. He joins the others and takes Paul's hand. Paul nods and takes Albertine's. They watch as Su Lin goes round to the open side of the pyramid. She ducks down, though she has no need to do so, and vanishes from sight.

'OK!' she calls. 'Close your eyes. Use all your power. Try to hear me. Right?'

The three children nod and close their eyes. They frown. Albertine's hand tightens trembling about

Paul's. The only sounds are those of Paul's grinding teeth and Albertine's increasingly heavy breathing through her nose.

At last, as though at a signal, their grips relax. Albertine sweeps the hair back off her brow. She shakes her head. 'No!' she calls. 'It's the pyramid! We can't hear a thing! We must ask Chocky about it. Come on. Su Lin. Let's finish this lot. It's nearly lunchtime!' She turns back to the table.

'Su Lin?' Paul stays staring at the pyramid, then, more urgently, 'Su Lin?'

'Come on, Su Lin.' Mike skips over to the pyramid.

'Su Lin?' Paul whispers again. He steps forward.

At the same moment, Albertine turns. Her eyes are wide. She drops the screwdriver with a clatter.

'Hey!' Mike stops. Paul is suddenly at his side. 'Hey, Su Lin! What's happened? Here, Paul, Albertine, give me a hand.'

'Oh, no!' Albertine yaps. She bends to grab one of the lifeless arms. Mike takes the other. Together they drag Su Lin out and round into the centre of the room. Her eyes are closed. Her head lolls back. Her long black hair sprays out over the flagstones.

Albertine kneels at her head. 'She's still breathing ...' she pants. 'Oh, Chocky! Help! Please help us, Chocky!'

Paul runs to the door and calls up the stairs, 'Help! Quickly! Please, help!'

'Chocky, please!' She looks up over her shoulder. Tears fill her eyes and overflow. Her right hand holds Su Lin's wrist. 'Chocky?' Her keening rises to end on a little squeak like a whiplash. 'Oh, oh, Chocky!' she breathes. 'Thank goodness you're here. What's the matter with her?'

A light moves down from the wall to Su Lin's head. For a second, it seems to fall on Su Lin's face.

'She will be all right. Do not worry. I will wake her up,' says Chocky.

Su Lin opens her eyes at the very moment at which Meyer and Mrs Gibson rush into the room. 'What is it?' Meyer pants. He is at Su Lin's side in two strides. 'Is she all right?'

Su Lin blinks. For a moment, there is panic in her eyes, then bewilderment. Then she fumbles for Mike's and Albertine's hands and she smiles. 'I'm OK.'

'But what happened, Chocky?' asks Albertine.

Meyer cocks his head to listen to something that he knows he cannot hear. 'What does she say?' he demands.

'Sh!' Albertine waves irritably. 'She says ... she says she is sorry. She should have warned us ...' Albertine straightens and helps Su Lin to her feet. 'We should be very careful when we go inside the pyramid,' she says. 'Even when it is not activated, it can be dangerous. The energy can overcome the mind, and since there is no way through the material, your mind can be trapped ... Really, Chocky?' she stares.

'What is it?' Mrs Gibson snaps. 'What does she say?'

Paul takes over. 'She says that even she has to be careful not to be caught inside a pyramid. The energy is just too powerful. Yes,' he nods to Chocky. 'And she says Su Lin needs rest.'

'Quite right, too,' says Meyer grimly. 'Come on, Su Lin. I'll give you a lift.' He bends to pick her up. 'You lot had better take the rest of the day off.'

Su Lin looks up at the wall and mutters sleepily. 'Thank you, Chocky.' Her cheek rests against Meyer's chest. Her breathing slows and steadies. A happy little smile touches her lips.

Paul sits reading by the empty grate. Mike is back at the piano doing a high-pitched Elton John imitation. Albertine is playing chess with Chocky. Chocky, says Albertine, thinks chess and cricket are the greatest innovations that she has encountered on Earth.

Albertine loses twice. She expects to lose, but not so rapidly or so ignominiously. 'I'm sorry, Chocky,' she says in response to some chiding, 'I don't seem able to concentrate.'

The cause of her distraction is soon apparent. Paul lays down his book, stands and stretches. He yawns with a very obvious sort of creaking sound. He says, 'rhubarbtiredrhubarb,' and saunters over to the door.

Albertine waits until she hears the Yale latch click shut. She whispers something to Chocky, nods a couple of times and gets up. 'Think I'll have a bit of a rest too, Mike,' she says.

Mike interrupts a gravelly rendition of Benny and the Jets to stick up a thumb. 'Sure,' he winks.

Albertine opens the door just a crack. She peers through. It is a cool, colourless day. There is an icy edge to the air.

Paul is out of sight. Albertine opens the door quickly, slips out and closes it quietly behind her. She scampers down the steps and looks up the road. Paul is some two hundred yards away, near the junction with the main road. His left hand drags along the palings. He walks quickly and purposefully.

Albertine stays crouched behind the brick gatepost until, with a glance over his shoulder, Paul turns left into Trumpington Road. Then she moves.

Once on the main road, she clings close to the wall and the trees at her left. Twice Paul peers nervously backward. Twice he disappears from view. She has to run a few paces to catch up. He has just passed the Botanical Gardens when he crosses the road. Albertine remains on the left-hand pavement. She sees him turn right again as though to walk up Bateman Street, then immediately left again.

He is in Brookside. Again, he stops on the pavement and glances over his shoulder and Albertine has to try very hard to look like a tree trunk. Then he turns back, forces his hands into his pocket and trots up two steps to a dark blue door. He rings the bell.

Albertine starts to run. She is directly opposite when the door opens. A woman appears at the door. She is smiling. She hugs Paul. A blue taxi passes, then a motorbike with a noise like an angry cat, then another couple of cars. Albertine peers this way and that. The woman places her hands on Paul's shoulder as though to usher him in.

Dr Beatrice Liddle.

Albertine must have dropped her guard. She must have let fire a thought in her momentary bewilderment, for Paul turns and stands on the doorstep once more and his lips form the word, 'Albertine?'

Then he sees her.

Standing behind him, Liddle too sees Albertine on the other side of the road. A lorry thunders past. Albertine blinks away the smoke and the dust. Liddle is beckoning to her.

When there is a gap in the traffic, Albertine crosses the road slowly. She stands at the foot of the steps and stares up at Paul. One corner of her mouth is tugged into her cheek in a humourless, sceptical smile. She nods slowly.

'Albertine,' Liddle nods back, but quickly, accepting the situation, 'well, I suppose you'd better come inside.'

Liddle's sitting-room is white. The furniture is all white or shiny black or tubular steel. There is a pale fawn rug on the bare floorboards and there is japonica in a vase on the low white coffee-table. There are no family photographs on the desk, just piles of print-outs and stellar charts and calculations, no novels or biographies in the steel bookcases, just big flat-backed files in white or black.

'Albertine . . .' Paul starts. He stands close to Liddle.

'Is this where you've been coming, then?'

Paul nods.

'But why, Paul? Why here?'

'Why not?' Liddle says briskly. 'He is my son.'

Albertine sits rather suddenly on the crumpled black chair. For a moment or two, she does not look very intelligent. 'Your son?' she murmurs, then, grasping the gist of the thing, 'You mean – you're Paul's mother?'

'As always, my dear,' Liddle smiles, not unpleasantly, 'your logic is impeccable.'

'Yes,' Albertine shakes herself. 'Not a very bright observation, was it, but . . .' She waves her arms as though attempting to scoop the various disparate strands of thought into one coherent ball.

'But why haven't we the same names?' Liddle supplies. 'Simple enough. Paul's father and I are divorced. I prefer to use my own name.' She too sits. She pats the sofa at her side. Paul joins her and takes her hand. 'As you know,' Liddle continues, 'Paul has been living with his father. We thought it best when we split up. He can give him more time. I – well, I'm afraid I get too tied up in my work. It's wrong, I know, but . . .' she shrugs.

'Has Paul been telling you about our work?'

Paul opens his mouth eagerly. His mother lays her right hand over his. 'Yes,' she says, 'yes, he has. And it sounds amazing.'

Albertine is suspicious again. Her lower jaw thrusts forward. 'Was that your idea, then? To get him in with us so that you could find out what we were up to?'

'No, no,' Liddle soothes. 'First it was his father's idea, then, by the sound of things, it was your friend Chocky's. I knew nothing about it. If I had, I'd have done my best to prevent it. I can assure you. Then, at any rate,' she adds gently. 'Now, I'm not so sure.'

'Oh? And why is that?'

'Because at the time I did not believe a single word of your projected research.'

'But you do now?'

'Yes. Yes, I do. I know that Paul would never lie to me. And besides – well, I suppose I owe it to you to tell you – there is something more.' She pats Paul's hand and stands again. She strolls over to the white trestle table which serves as her desk. She looks down at some charts, then up at the sky. 'I'm glad you've come here,' she tells the window, 'because it gives me a chance to say that I'm sorry.'

'What for?' Albertine's voice is quiet now.

'For refusing to believe you. And for making such a fuss about the computer program. You see, my dear, you were absolutely right about those messages from another civilisation – and I am well on the way to being able to prove it.' She turns. She is silhouetted now against the light from the street. 'I was on the verge of it all the time, but I never realised. I never would have realised either. I am trained not to think in terms of the improbable possible. I never would have allowed myself to realise if you hadn't come along.'

'And Chocky, of course,' Paul says, suddenly cheery.

'Of course,' Liddle smiles.

'But that is marvellous!' Albertine stands. She walks over to within five feet of Liddle where she leans back on her desk. 'Are you going to announce it? Are you going to publish?'

'Not *just* yet,' Liddle wags a finger playfully. 'I've still got a tremendous amount of work to do before I dare publish. Otherwise, I'm afraid, the scientific world would react in just the same way as I did to you.'*

Albertine nods. 'Just one other thing,' she says. 'I've got to ask you.' She looks into Liddle's eyes. 'Have you told anyone anything about our work? Have you mentioned anything to anyone? Anyone at all?'

Liddle steps forwards. She takes Albertine's hands. 'No,' she says solemnly, 'Please believe me, Albertine. I promise I've told no one anything. I swear.'

Albertine looks hard at her, then nods and smiles. She returns the pressure of the hands. 'All right,' she says. 'I believe you.'

'Paul was so much happier after that,' Albertine

* *Some Researches Into Rhythmical Signals from Twin Binaries in an Extra-Galactic Nebula* by Dr Beatrice Liddle, Fellow of Churchill College, Cambridge. Cambridge University Press, 1988 (£23). *Signals from the Stars* by Beatrice Liddle and Mark Daniel. Methuen, 1989 (£8.95).

wrote. 'All suspicion was gone, and we were able to get on with our work as a family again. Dr Liddle is not the easiest of people. I think she finds it a little difficult to be open and affectionate, to smile or to touch or to share things, but I have come quite to like her. It is just that she is completely taken up with her work.

'Within a couple of days, we had completed the pyramid. With the sphere positioned as before, in one of the angles, the pyramid would stand unsupported on its apex. The world's first cosmic powerpack.

'Of course, we could have published there and then, but Chocky wanted us to go further. The next stage was to link our power source to existing technology – to learn the practical applications of our pyramid. This was far more theoretical, so it was back to the schoolroom for all of us as Chocky taught us, day after day in total silence.

'It is quite astonishing how stupid intelligent people can be, especially when they want to believe something. We had no inkling that we were being tricked until one day Mrs Gibson went off "on business" to London. She returned all full of bustle and self-importance and summoned a meeting in the sitting-room after supper . . .'

Chapter ten

'I've told my chief all about your success with the pyramid,' Mrs Gibson says as she perches on the piano stool, 'and you'll be pleased to hear that he is most impressed.'

'I'd be astonished were he not,' says Meyer drily. 'So there'll be no problems over finance for the next stage?'

'No, no. Absolutely not. No problems whatever. I've been instructed to make sure that you have everything that you need.'

'Phew!' Mike parodies relief.

'After all, we recognise that your work is vitally important for the country . . .'

'Hey! Hey! Hold on!' Mike holds up a chubby pink palm. 'Which country you talking about, man?'

'Why, this one, of course,' Mrs Gibson says blithely, then, realising her mistake. 'And thus, of course, it will benefit the Western Alliance as a whole . . .'

'Yes, but Chocky isn't interested in any one country or any one alliance,' says Albertine from deep in an armchair.

'No, of course not!' snaps Mrs Gibson. 'We appreciate that. Of course we do! But of course, you must also remember that if your work were to get into the wrong hands, it would be a terrible thing for the entire world, you understand?'

'Of course we understand.' There is a warning note in Albertine's voice. 'We have some experience of such matters.'

'Good,' efficiently, then 'Good!' patronisingly. 'So you will understand how important security is going to be now that you have reached this advanced stage.'

'Yeees,' Meyer is suspicious. 'Naturally we don't want anybody trying to sabotage what the children and Chocky are doing . . .'

'Precisely. Good. Splendid. So I've made arrangements for you all to move to new quarters, somewhere safer, you know? And you'll all be very comfortable and properly looked after and protected. Right?'

'Wrong.' Mike swaggers over and thumps the piano lid. 'We're happy here and we're staying here. We can look after ourselves, thank you.'

'Hear hear!'

'Yeah.'

'Yes. Why should we move?'

'Ah, ah.' Mrs Gibson stands and looks at each of the children in turn. She gives a conciliatory sort of smile, but her eyebrows rise. 'That's all very well, but there's more than that at stake, isn't there, mmm? You see, we have come to realise just how important your discoveries could be in the realm of defence.'

'Defence?' Meyer growls.

'Which,' says Su Lin calmly, 'can usually be translated as attack, right?'

'You mean military-type defence?' Mike gives her a hard stare.

'Er, yes, of course.'

'No,' says Albertine simply.

'You are working for the government,' Mrs Gibson is getting riled now, 'and what you are doing is covered by the Official Secrets Act.'

'Ah, Mrs Gibson, Mrs Gibson,' Meyer leans back

in his chair and chuckles, 'think what you are saying. The Official Secrets Act is a bad and consistently discredited law. Neither the public nor the high court has much time for it even when applied to senior civil servants, so how do you think you'd fare with a group of public-spirited children, eh? And exactly what do you think you could do? Lock the children up? I think you'd find that very difficult. Not only would the press hound you, but they can open any door without keys. And even if you could manage that, you can't lock up their minds. They could still talk to their friends all over the world. And then there's Chocky herself. What in the world do you propose to do to Chocky with your Secrets Act?'

'Yes,' says Paul. He sounds so uncharacteristically assertive that everyone turns to look at him. 'And how do you know that Chocky hasn't already got other children working as we are – in Russia or China or Japan or South America. I was reading about that the other day – how there seems to be an evolutionary clock so that as soon as one member of a species thinks of something new, others, sometimes many miles away, think of it too. Our knowledge has entered the world now. You can't get rid of it. I mean – well – um, sorry.'

'No!' Meyer nods. 'Well said, Paul! You see what you're up against, Mrs Gibson?'

'If you try and stop us,' says Su Lin, cool as ever, 'Chocky will simply go somewhere else. Like Russia, perhaps.'

'So that's it, I'm afraid, Mrs Gibson,' Albertine smiles politely. 'Chocky's knowledge isn't for any one side. It's for everybody. It's for the whole world.'

Mrs Gibson inhales through her teeth, then rolls over her lips to cover them tightly. She glares at Albertine, then at Mike, who beams back at her and gives a little wave. 'I shall have to speak to the General about this,' she says in a rapid monotone, and sits.

'The General?' Meyer pulls himself up from his chair and leans on the piano lid. 'And what, pray, is a General doing in the Ministry of Science?'

'Yes,' Mrs Gibson studies her nails, 'well. It's not . . . I don't actually work for the Ministry of Science. Not as such.'

Albertine throws herself forward from her chair and joins her father at the piano. Her hair shoots forward from her forehead. 'You mean,' her eyes flash, 'you mean you lied to us!'

'I had to, my dear,' Mrs Gibson gulps uncomfortably. 'I didn't want to, but one has to do a lot of unpleasant things in order to ensure the security and welfare of our people. The department that I work for is very secret.'

Meyer puts an arm around Albertine's shoulders. 'Well,' he says firmly, 'I suggest that you return to your General, whoever he may be, and tell him what we say. We will not have this work used in what you refer to as "defence". We refuse to restrict it to one country or one culture, and if he tries to force the issue, the children or Chocky will simply pass the information to their friends, who may or may not be as benevolent as us. Understood?'

There are large red spots on Mrs Gibson's cheeks. 'I understand,' she twangs.

'Good. And now, children, I think that it's time for bed. We still have a lot of work to do. Good night, Mrs Gibson – if that is your name.'

'Good *night*,' says Mrs Gibson sourly. As the door shuts, she brings her fist down on the bass keys in a terrible discord.

*

Mrs Gibson is up and gone before the others come down to breakfast. She returns two days later.

Paul is alone. He sits curled up on the sofa, munching crisps and reading a book. Occasionally as he turns a page, he glances at his watch.

A taxi pulls up outside. A woman's voice is just heard above the feverish heartbeat of the engine. The gate creaks. Footfalls on the gravel echo Paul's chewing. For a moment the birdsong is amplified, then muted as the door swings open and shut. The double click of heels on the tiles tells Paul who is there. He sighs and deliberately concentrates even harder on his book.

'Hello.' Mrs Gibson puts her head around the door.

Paul does not look up. 'Hello.'

'All on your own, then?'

'The others have gone on a picnic.' He turns a page.

'What, and left you out?' Mrs Gibson tut-tuts.

Paul looks up now. She is standing by the arm of the sofa, just two feet away from him. Her eyes are very bright and birdlike. 'No,' he says, 'I'm going to see my mother, but it isn't time yet.'

'Ah, I see. I wonder if you could give me a hand then.'

'What for?'

'I wanted to have another quick look at the sphere – the energy collector, you know. Just a matter of checking its dimensions. Silly me. I'm afraid I must have typed them out wrong. My two reports don't tally.'

'It's in the pyramid,' says Paul.

'Yes, I know. I don't like to tamper with your things. I just wondered if you would get it out for me, just for a second.'

Paul shrugs. 'OK. I suppose so,' he frowns as he walks to the door. 'I suppose it's all right . . .'

'There it is. It's easy to get the side off. It just slots in. Look.' Paul releases the catch and pulls at the triangular face. Suddenly the low hum of the sphere fills the room and sets the walls singing. He lays the face carefully down on the flagstones. 'There,' he points.

Inside the pyramid, the sphere gives off an even glow. The reflective pyramids all about it flicker like tinsel on the tree. Paul is suddenly aware of the silence throughout the house. 'I – I ought to be going . . .'

'Yes. But could you just reach the sphere out for me, my dear?' Her hand pushes gently but insistently at the small of his back. 'I do hate to touch these things. They're so heavy and I'm so clumsy.'

Paul looks up at her. He gives a quick, apprehensive little grin. 'All right,' he nods, 'but I must hurry.'

'Of course. Just fetch it out for me.'

'OK. I'll fetch it . . .'

He crouches down and steps into the pyramid.

He hears a grunt. He turns, one arm raised. Suddenly a big triangle is blocking out the light like a train hurtling into a tunnel towards him. He yelps and ducks, then barges at the final face as the lines of white light narrow and vanish. The wall gives, but the pressure against him is too great. He hears a quick, deep breath from outside, the 'click' as the clasp is fastened. 'Let me out!' he screams, but the words splash back over him and fade to meld with the humming of the sphere. 'Let me out, let me out, let me *out*!'

He hammers at the wall with his fist, rests his head on his forearm and a sob bubbles up from deep inside him. 'Let me out!'

The strength seems to be drawn from his body in waves. It's like sloughing off layers of skin. The cold runs down from his head to his feet, from his head to his feet. Everything fades then save the humming of the sphere. It grows louder and louder until it fills his head and blocks out thought and his brain is a great soft balloon and someone is pumping water into it until it pushes against the fragile fabric of his skull and either the balloon or the skull must burst.

He does not know whether he is still screaming. Something is. He does not know that his knees have buckled or that he has slashed his forehead as he fell. There is no top to the pyramid. There are no sides. The disco pulsing of the light in the walls grows dim and goes out. There is no more power.

His last thought is the old idealist's problem. If a bomb goes off in the desert and no one hears it, is there sound? If a boy sends out signals of anguish and they merely echo and jangle in his own head, is there pain?

And outside the pyramid, a woman's voice calls, 'Chocky! Chocky! Come and help Paul! Chocky! Chocky!'

Somewhere, Paul knows, light shines through his closed eyelids. There is a quick gust of cool air. And Chocky is with him. The woman has summoned Chocky. Chocky is in the pyramid with him. All will be well. Chocky's cool light fills his brain. Chocky is in the pyramid with him. Chocky is . . .

'No, Chocky!' a distant voice yells from the back of his brain. 'Look out!'

Then the pyramid sucks up the air in one last breath and there is darkness once again.

There is a red gingham cloth. There is chicken and smoked trout and lettuce and tomatoes and basil and warm grass and ice cold lemonade. The punts are moored askew beneath a willow. The giggles and guffaws of undergraduates float downstream. Occasionally another punt passes close by with a slow and regular gulping.

Meyer and the three children doze.

Suddenly Albertine sits up and rubs her eyes. Mike, who is actually asleep, twitches and stiffens like a dying dog. Su Lin sits up, clutches her belly and jacknifes.

'What?' Albertine frowns.

Su Lin closes her eyes. She links forefingers and thumbs. She is looking for something. She shakes her head and smiles. The something is not there. Nothing remains to worry them.

They doze again.

The Gores have two apartments on the same floor. One is home, the other is Matthew's studio. Matthew is moving with some difficulty from the one to the other. At last he solves the problem. If he puts the glass of milk under one elbow, the toast *and* the paintbrush in his mouth and the portfolio under the other arm, he can just reach up with the keys to unlock the door.

His studio was a called a 'studio apartment' before he moved in, but that was just estate-agent speak for a bedsit. A grand, north-facing bedsit, it is true, but a lot of work had to be done before it was truly worthy of its grandiose name. They stripped it down to bare boards and plain white plaster and they knocked two iron-checkered windows into one huge sliding frame which runs the length of the room.

Matthew is impatient to be back at his painting again. He makes it a rule to stop work of an evening at a point where he most longs to go on, so that his dreams will be full of his painting and he will awake itching to continue. He hates a blank mind and a blank canvas.

His mother has taken Polly off to school. She will be back soon, but she will not disturb him, save perhaps to bring in a cup of tea at some stage later in the day. His father, who has been working harder than ever since they arrived here, left still earlier. Matthew is deliciously alone.

He squirts paint on to his palette and works it with smooth, broad movements of the wrist. He is applying the paint directly on to the canvas with the palette knife. His painting is dark, yet full of opalescent moonlight. It is clear that his technique with oils has imporved. His every movement is more confident, his every dab on the canvas more authoritative.

He steps back and squints at the painting over the knife.

Suddenly his eyes widen. 'Oh . . .' he whines on a rising, questioning tone. The palette knife drops from his fingers. The palette itself lands flat on the boards with a report like a rifle shot. Matthew leans on the bench at his side for support, then wheels round on his arm and slumps down. 'Oh, no . . .' His face emerges flushed from behind his trembling fingers. What starts as a whisper becomes a scream. 'Al-ber-*tine*!'

'Something's wrong,' says Albertine suddenly, and her face is white.

118

'What?' Meyer looks up from the packing of the picnic basket. All the children are busy gathering up the debris of the meal, folding cloths and napkins.

'Something's wrong. Matthew . . .'

'What's wrong with Matthew?' Meyer frowns.

'No!' she snaps, 'no, it's nothing wrong with *Matthew*. Matthew knows . . . Something's wrong *here*, in *Cambridge*. Come on! *Quickly!*'

She drops the tablecloth and starts to run up the riverbank. Su Lin follows almost immediately. Mike looks down at Meyer, then up at the girls. He too drops the rubbish bag in his hands, lowers his head and scurries off after them. 'But the punts!' Meyer shouts after them. 'The picnic!'

'Come on!' Albertine's voice is already distant. With flailing arms, she turns on to the high metal footbridge that leads to the Fort St George and Midsummer Common. Meyer throws down the picnic basket and curses. 'Oh, God!' he mutters. 'Why can't I have normal children?'

He too starts to run.

They catch a taxi at the bus station. It takes six minutes to get back home. Before the car stops, Albertine has the door open. She throws herself out and careers up the steps. Su Lin and Mike follow close behind. Meyer is left to frown and grumble and pay the taxi-driver.

Albertine fumbles with the keys in the lock. She curses. 'Paul!' she yells up at the first-floor windows. She flings open the door. Her voice echoes around the hall. 'Paul!'

She charges into the living-room then straight out again. 'The cellar . . .' she gasps. Meyer slams the front door shut behind him. He follows the children down the cellar stairs. Even before he reaches the bottom, the cries of dismay have told him the story.

'The pyramid!'

'Oh, no, not again!'

'No,' Albertine looks about her wildly. 'It's more serious than that – I don't know! I don't understand!'

'It's Mrs Gibson,' says Su Lin. 'I know it is. I bet she was the one who pinched the first sphere.'

'Yes,' Meyer nods. 'I'm afraid so. If they can't have the energy collector for their purposes, no one can have it. She's been the jinx on the whole project.'

'But she's crazy,' says Mike. 'I mean, she can't stop us like this. We just build another . . .'

'Chocky?' Albertine calls. 'Chocky?'

'. . . I mean, it's all in the computer memory, anyhow . . .'

'It's not,' says Su Lin dully. 'It's been wiped clean.'

'Everything?' Meyer moans.

'Everything.'

'Chocky! Chocky!'

'What the devil does the woman think she's playing at?'

'Yeah, well,' Mike stamps. 'Chocky doesn't need a computer either.'

'Chocky!' Albertine wails, 'Chocky!'

'Maybe Paul knows something about it,' says Meyer.

'I'll ask him,' Mike closes his eyes. 'Oh, hang it! Now *he's* not answering.'

'Why does he have to switch off like that?' Su Lin sighs.

'He might not be back for hours.'

'Chocky! Please!' Albertine sobs.

Her voice clangs back at her from the corners like a peal of bells.

The telephone warbles. Meyer leaps across the room as though to wring its neck. 'Yes? Ah, Dr Liddle,' he sighs. 'No . . . no, he's not here . . . but he should have been with you hours ago . . . Oh, God, I don't know what's happening. The pyramid's gone . . . Yes. We were out on the river. It's that woman Gibson . . . Now wait. You stay there by the phone. We'll come over as soon as you hear anything and . . . yes, I promise. The moment we find out . . . yes. Fine. It'll be all right. I'm sure it will . . .'

'Chocky!' Albertine angrily punches the tears away on her sleeve. 'Chocky! Why won't she answer?'

'Chocky!' Su Lin takes Albertine's hand.

'Chocky!' Mike yells as though calling a disobedient dog.

'Why isn't she here?' Meyer asks. 'We need her. God, do we need her. That was Beatrice Liddle. Paul has vanished too. Why doesn't she answer you?'

'Maybe she can't hear us,' offers Mike.

'Don't be silly,' Su Lin says impatiently: 'Chocky can always hear us. Particularly when we call really hard like this.'

'So maybe she's gone home.'

'Why?' Albertine stares. 'Why would she do that? She just wouldn't . . .'

'Unless . . .' Su Lin muses.

All three pairs of eyes turn on her. 'What?'

'Well, you remember how the pyramid affected us, how we couldn't hear Mike calling from inside and I sort of fainted . . . ?'

'Yes,' says Albertine pensively. 'Yes . . .'

'And Chocky warned us then, don't you remember? She said even she had to be very careful not to get caught in a pyramid.'

'And,' Meyer thuds, 'Mrs Gibson was standing right here.'

Chapter eleven

It takes Matthew just twenty-five minutes to do what must be done.

He takes his passport and his bank-book from his mother's bureau and sits down briefly to write.

> Dear Mum and Dad,
> Don't worry. This isn't the classic goodbye, I've-gone-to-join-the-Legion letter Something is badly wrong in Cambridge. I'm getting all sorts of confused signals from Albertine and the others and neither they nor I can find Chocky. Chocky just isn't there anymore. Maybe because I've had her with me longest, her absence is like a painful presence, if you know what I mean, and I know that she is trying desperately to reach me.
> I have no time. Sorry. I think we need our combined strength to solve the problem. Albertine says they need me. I'll pay the fare out of the exhibition money, and I'll call you this evening from Cambridge.
> Don't worry, I'll be all right.
> Love,
> Matthew

He changes into clean jeans, a white shirt and a blue crew-neck sweater. He does not bother to pack, just shoves a toothbrush into his coat pocket and leaves.

A yellow cab takes him from the bank to Kennedy airport. A few heads turn as he boards Concorde just fifty minutes later. It may be just because he is fourteen years old and travelling alone. It may be because his face is streaked with tears.

'That's right,' Meyer raps into the telephone, 'Gibson. Pru – Prudence, I suppose – Gibson. Yes. You're sure? Thank you. Yes. Good evening.' He replaces the receiver and turns to the waiting children. 'The Ministry has never heard of her.'

'We need Chocky,' Albertine speaks like an automaton that needs winding. 'We need Chocky so much. If only . . .'

'Yeah,' says Mike, 'if only.'

'Well,' Meyer slaps his thigh, 'I'll go and organise some supper. We can't think without fuel.'

There is silence in the living-room for a minute or more. Then Su Lin's clear voice says, 'We need another Chocky.'

'Mmm.' Albertine sighs. Her head jerks up. 'Or Chocky's parent!'

The children exchange rapid glances.

'Do you think we could?' asks Su Lin.

'We can only try.'

'Yeah, I mean, Chocky did say sending your mind through space was not that much different from our own telepathy.'

'OK,' says Su Lin, 'let's try it. Who should do it?'

'Albertine. She's had most practice.'

'All right.' Albertine takes a deep breath, happy at least that there is something to do. 'Let's get ourselves ready.'

She pushes aside the armchair to make space. All

three children sit cross-legged and face each other on the tree-of-life rug. Their hands rest upon their knees. Three pyramids, then, in a triangle.

'Clear our minds,' intones Mike.

'Concentrate ... concentrate ...'

'Ready,' says Albertine. 'Now ...'

'It's hard to explain how it feels,' Albertine told me in our only face to face interview. 'It is travelling of a sort, and yes, you do get a sensation of movement, of passing things, you know? But the things are not specific, and time is all mixed up, so you're not travelling at any one speed or at any speed at all ... Oh, I don't know. At any one moment, you're moving, but everything that you have already passed and everything that you are going to encounter is present and can be summoned closer. I'll tell you what it's like. It's like a guide book. You have the whole world there in that book, but you can't take it in all at once so you choose to organise the data in terms of progress. You start at page one and move on through. But in fact, you can always jump on ahead or go backwards wherever you feel like it. Page one is as present as page 100. Oh, dear. You don't understand a word I'm saying, do you?'

'Well, sort of,' I said, 'I mean, it's not easy to explain because we haven't got words for what you're talking about, but I take your point about time. But you say you pass things. What sort of things? I mean, are we talking about stars and planets and things, or what?'

She screwed up her face and made a groaning noise. 'Well ... yes, sort of, but no. I mean, I thought of them as stars, but in fact I suppose they were *emanations*, like Chocky in a sense, only these were not

124

all emanations from intelligent life forms, or even from creatures that were still alive. I suppose you could call them ghosts, really. Oh, I don't know, It's confusing. I'm so bad at explaining things like this . . .'

'It's no good,' Albertine's shoulders droop. 'It's no good. We just aren't strong enough.'

'Perhaps if Paul were here . . .?' She shakes her head, once more, dejected. 'No, but wait! Matthew is coming!' She leaps to her feet and claps. 'Matthew is coming! Matthew is coming! He's the best of us all. We can do it! I know we can!'

Heathrow to Liverpool Street. It's dark now.

'I'm here, Albertine. Hold on, I'm here.'

'What's that, then, squire?' The taxi-driver's head swivels like a parrot's.

'Oh, nothing,' says Matthew. 'Please. Be as quick as you can . . .'

Beatrice Liddle looks very old. Her eyelids droop. They show a lot of red. Her usually neat hair is a mess. Her skin is as white and lifeless as marshmallow.

She inhales deep on her cigarette and releases it with a little 'Pht'. The ashtray on the arm of her chair already contains some nine, ten butts. A thick strand of smoke hangs above the waiting children's heads.

When she speaks, her voice is very deep. 'But this detaching your minds, this travelling outside yourself,' she croaks, 'it may be all right for Chocky, but isn't it dangerous for you?'

'No more dangerous than it is for Chocky and Paul to stay inside that pyramid,' says Albertine. 'We've got to try. It's our only hope.'

125

'Makes sense,' Meyer nods. He has not taken to smoking, but he has paced a lot, until the children yelled at him to stop, and now he sits at the desk and taps his teeth with his gold pen. 'It's the only solution that I can think of.'

Albertine pulls herself to her feet. A little smile plays on her lips. 'He's here,' she says quietly. She walks out into the hall. On the doorstep, she breathes in deep and gazes up at the stars. Somewhere up there is Chocky's parent, somewhere, many light years away and unaware, is the solution to the problems of a few young humans.

Albertine likes looking at the stars. She likes the concept of infinite expansion, the incomprehensibly vast figures which spring to her mind when she reflects upon the greatness of the visible universe and the many huge spinning galaxies way beyond our own. They force her to acknowledge the insignificance of her endeavours and yet, paradoxically, the immense importance of any creature who had survived in so treacherous a tide of hydrogen. To give cosmic energy to the world is as little, and as much, as to bring some small comfort to your own tiny family in a great grimy city.

Here, then, with a muttering of cab engines, comes Matthew, at 1,000 miles an hour around the polar axis, at 70,000 miles an hour around the sun, at 1,000,000 miles an hour around the Galaxy and at thirty miles an hour along the pocked tarmac surface of Chaucer Road.

She is there on the pavement to open the door when the taxi stops. 'Thank heavens you're here,' she says warmly. 'We need you, so much.'

'I know,' he manages some sort of smile of greeting. 'I hope I'm not too late.' He pays the driver and turns to climb the steps with her. 'I find it so difficult to cope with the emptiness of . . .'

'I know,' she says briefly. 'Come on.'

She shows him into the living-room. Meyer strides forward, his hand extended. 'Matthew!' he cries.

Su Lin nods familiarly at Matthew as though she's known him all her life.

'Su Lin,' says Matthew simply.

'Hi, Matthew.'

'Hi, Mike.'

'And this is Dr Liddle,' says Meyer, 'Paul's mother.'

'Hello,' Liddle exhales twin columns of smoke and briefly lays a hand on Matthew's forearm. 'Thank you for coming,' she says.

'I had to. Hello.'

'You know what's going on, then?' asks Meyer.

'Yes, I think so.'

'You see, the three of us just aren't strong enough,' Su Lin explains. 'But we thought that with you too . . .'

'I think it might work,' Matthew nods.

'You aren't too tired after your trip?'

'No,' he grins, 'I had a good long sleep. Let's get on with it.'

Liddle gets up wearily and moves over to the piano stool in the corner. She exchanges a worried look with Meyer. He just shrugs and nods and gives her a consoling smile.

The children sit facing one another once again. Matthew takes Albertine's hand and closes his eyes tightly shut. The others follow suit. 'Let's go,' says Matthew quietly.

This time, it seems to last for many minutes. The contours of strain on the children's faces vanish as they seem to find some solace, return as they set off on their search again. A little tic beats in Mike's forehead. Occasionally, Albertine's lips twitch like a fishing line at a bite. Only Matthew and Su Lin appear composed and serene. Sometimes Matthew even grins with pleasure as he finds some delight on his wanderings, then the pioneer frown returns. Move on. We must move on . . .

The silence is broken at last by a common sigh. Again the tense bodies seem to collapse like stringless puppets.

'It's no use,' Albertine shakes her head fast.

'What is it?' Meyer squats. 'What's the matter?'

Liddle too comes over. She puts one hand on Mike's shoulder, one on Su Lin's. 'Are you all right, that's the main thing.'

'Yes,' Su Lin smiles weakly. 'We're fine.'

'You can't do it?' Meyer coaxes. 'You're still not strong enough?'

'Oh, it's not that,' says Matthew. 'We're easily strong enough. It's just . . .'

'What then?'

'It's just too big. There's just too much space. We're just aiming at random. It could take forever to find the right sector, let alone the right planet.' He grits his teeth and thumps the carpet. 'We don't even know where to begin.'

Hands are loosened. The children sit slumped and alone now, suddenly pathetic after the unified strength which had been apparent even to earthbound watchers. Meyer stands and resumes his pacing. Liddle hugs first Mike, then Su Lin. She blinks away tears as she stands.

'Hold it!' she announces suddenly. 'We do!'

'We do what?' Matthew blinks up at her.

'We do know where to start. Exactly where! Come on!'

'Where are we going?'

'Think, young Albertine, think!' she reverts from habit to her usual sardonic tone. 'Use that infant prodigy brain. We *know* where Chocky's parent lives, don't we?'

'We do ...?' Albertine looks obtuse, then, 'The *telescope*!'

'Go to the top of the class and jump off,' Liddle shrugs on a coat. 'Of course the telescope. Come on. We'll all have to squeeze into my car. Let's go.'

Again now the circle is formed. The children practise deep breathing as Liddle checks out the coordinates and realigns the telescope antennae. 'There,' she says at last. 'That's it.'

'OK,' Matthew nods slowly. 'We can get there now. Ready?'

'Yes.'

'Yes.'

'Yes. Let's go.'

'Oh!' Albertine squeaks, 'Oh! What ...?'

Her face twists in what looks like agony. Her trunk rocks back and forth. Meyer lopes forward. He is about to speak, but Liddle checks him with a hand.

Matthew is smiling blissfully and nodding. Albertine's lips start to move. Muttered words force their way through her teeth. 'Chocky ... need Chocky's parent ... Earth ... my planet ... Earth ... please help ... trapped ... cosmic energy pyramid ... please help ... please ... yes ... yes ... yes ...'

Her cheeks twitch and strain. The tic at Mike's temple pulses so hard and fast that it seems that the blood vessel there must burst. Even Su Lin looks as though she is about to cry and her body trembles. Only Matthew keeps smiling, as though by his pleasure in the experience he is sustaining all the others. He too mutters once, but all he says is 'Chocky's parent', in a tone of infinite satisfaction.

'Can't . . . can't hold on any longer . . .' Albertine pants. 'Please help . . . please help . . . aah-oh!'

Her head falls on her breast. She puffs out air like a boxer after a good punch has gone home to the solar plexus. Su Lin shudders visibly. She throws herself back on the cold tiled floor. Mike mops his sweat-shiny brow and gasps, 'Oh, man!'

Matthew stays exactly where he was. His eyes remain closed. The smile stays on his face. Liddle shakes his shoulder. 'Are you all right?' she demands.

'Yes.' Matthew's eyes open. Beatrice Liddle will maintain that they are different eyes from those which closed a few minutes and a few light years before. 'Yes, we're fine,' he says.

'Thank God,' says Meyer. 'Thank God, but did you . . . ?'

'Yes, Daddy,' pants Albertine. 'We did it . . .'

'You mean you actually got through to Chocky's people?' Liddle shakes her head, incredulous.

'Yes. But not on their own planet. This was the colony.'

'So what happens now?'

'They can't come themselves,' says Matthew, 'because they don't know where we are. But they're going to communicate with their home planet and try to find Chocky's parent.'

'And we?' Liddle asks. 'What are we meant to do?'

'Nothing,' replies Albertine. 'All we can do is sit and wait . . .'

*

They are sitting and waiting. Occasionally Liddle gets up to announce that she is going to call the police, only to be reminded that she will have a hard time persuading them of the truth of her tale. Occasionally Meyer thinks of another old friend who once worked in some hush-hush capacity for the Ministry of This and That and hunts for his number and calls him to ask if he has ever heard of a Pru Gibson. Occasionally Su Lin and Mike argue about nothing in particular. Occasionally Matthew and Albertine take a walk in the garden to reminisce and to pretend that things are back to normal. But basically, they sit and wait.

It is just after eleven o'clock in the morning when their visitor arrives. The children are all talking at the same time and then suddenly at the same time they stiffen and fall silent.

'What?' Meyer barks.

'This is it,' says Albertine, sphinxlike.

'Yes,' Matthew nods, then calls, 'Who are you?'

'I – am – Chocky's – parent.'

Chapter twelve

'I didn't believe it at first,' Meyer told me, 'even though I'd lived with the knowledge of Chocky for years. When I heard that strange, tinny voice and saw this light-ball growing in the room, I looked around for something to explain it, something logical. I know it sounds crazy, but I really did. And Beatrice Liddle, she saw it too, and she looked like a cartoon character, you know? Eyes wide open, mouth wide open, ashtray falling from the arm of her chair. Only goes to show what hidebound fools we so-called adults can be. The children were wise enough to know the thing for what it was, to accept it . . .'

'Tell me what happened to Chocky.'
'She has been trapped.' Albertine's voice wavers and there are tears in her eyes, but she explains very slowly and precisely. 'She has been trapped in a cosmic energy pyramid.'
'What is that?'
'Just a moment. I'll make the shape in my mind.' She closes her eyes. Her hands flutter as though moulding.
'Ah, yes. I understand. Chocky taught you how to make this?'
'Yes.'
'And now she is caught inside it?'
'With my son,' interposes Liddle.
'Your son?'
'Her child,' explains Matthew.

The ball of light moves over to Liddle and for a moment entirely encloses her head. Liddle nods and smiles. When the light moves back to it's place in the centre of the room, she sits up straight, her weariness forgotten. Her eyes give out more light.

'If they are not released soon, they will both die.'

'That's why we called you,' says Matthew. 'We need your help.'

'Where is the pi . . .?'

'Pyramid,' Matthew supplies.

'We don't know,' says Mike.

'We need your help in finding it. Can you do that?'

'I do not know. A pyramid holds all its energy inside. That is its purpose. The other collector, however, is different.'

'You mean the sphere?' Albertine closes her eyes again. 'Like this?'

'Yes, the sphere sends out energy. That is why it goes inside the pyramid. I could find that, if it is not inside a pyramid now.'

'It is,' Meyer moans.

'But hold on.' Albertine gets out of her chair and stands in the centre of the room. Her face is very close to the ball of light. 'There is another sphere. It too was stolen, probably by the same people. If you could find that . . .'

'I will try. Wait.'

The ball of light shivers and fades like the clash of a cymbal.

Chocky's parent returns after two, maybe three minutes. Everyone stands together now in the middle of the room. Everyone touches someone else. Hands hold hands, arms hold tight around shoulders. Everyone is tense.

'D – did you find it,' Albertine asks politely.

'Yes. The sphere is at a place called J – J – Jarrett.'

'I know it,' Meyer nods grimly. 'It's a military base.'

'It appears that some of your fellow humans are not even as intelligent as you. The leader of this Jarrett community has white hair. He could not speak very well when I spoke to him. He took a lot of medicaments and lost control of his urinary tract . . .'

Matthew laughs. 'You're as bad as Chocky,' he says affectionately.

'Is it far from here?' Albertine asks her father.

'No. About half an hour. Out on the Cherry Hinton road.'

'Are they all right, though?' asks Liddle. 'Paul and Chocky, are they all right?'

'I do not know. I do not understand your time scale yet, so I cannot tell how long they have been inside. We may already be too late.'

It is Mike who breaks the hypnotic stillness. 'Come on!' he shouts. 'Let's get going!'

Suddenly the room is full of activity. Car keys jangle. Coats rustle.

'But what are you going to do when you get there?' Liddle bends to pick up her handbag.

'Leave that to us,' says Albertine.

'Don't worry,' adds Matthew. 'We'll manage.'

'You go for the police, Miss Liddle,' Meyer orders. 'Now. I'll take the kids. Meet us there as soon as you can.'

Meyer's car was not built for speed. It was not particularly built for comfort either, as Albertine, Mike and Su Lin discover as they sway and bump in unison, jammed tight together in the back seat. By dint of jumping traffic lights, ignoring pedestrian crossings and the greater part of the Highway Code with regard to Rights of Way, it is a mere twenty-two minutes before they catch sight of Jarrett.

They catch sight, more specifically, of a fence, about half a mile away up on their left. That's about all there is to be seen of Jarrett; a long, high, wire-netting fence which leans in at the top and is crowned with barbed wire. This fence, which is patrolled by uniformed guards with guns at their hips and Alsatians at their sides, surrounds a thirty acre compound of grass. A couple of buildings become visible as the car approaches the gates – a plain high cream building which looks like a warehouse, two or three long low cream billet huts with corrugated iron roofs – but most of Jarrett is grass.

To an alien like Chocky's parent, it must seem strange that so much security is devoted to the protection of an area of sheep-feed, until he notices the strange shapes of the grassy hills, the doors set into their sides. Whatever happens at Jarrett happens underground.

The car jolts to a halt and rocks before the great double gates. Meyer and the children are out before it has stopped rocking.

A guard stands on either side of the gates. One is black, the other white. Both carry small sub-machine guns with plastic stocks. A large, almost entirely black Alsatian crouches at the white man's side. The hairs on its neck bristle like a doormat.

'Get away from here!' the black man warns. The dog sinks lower. The guns rattle as they are unslung. 'This is government property. You keep away . . .'

The children exchange one of their secret, rapid glances. They turn back to face the sentries and their eyes turn to marble. The white guard frowns. He staggers backward. His colleague puts out a hand to support himself on the fence. 'Hey!' he says, 'What . . .?' Both men yawn. The guns slip from their hands and clatter to the ground. The dog yawns too.

The guards go down. They are still blinking and frowning as they fall to their knees. The black man is still trying to speak. His eyes are bemused and imploring, but not for long. His colleague is already stretched out full length on the tarmac. Now he too falls forward over his gun and lies still.

The dog's hackles are smoothed back as if by an invisible hand. It gets up and trots over to the fence. It strikes at it tentatively with its paw and pants contentedly.

The children smile.

'Now the gate,' says Meyer.

'But it's locked, man!' exclaims Mike.

Matthew and Albertine step forward. 'Remember?' he says with that sheepish grin.

Albertine nods. They have done this before. They hold hands and they stare at the lock. It whirrs and clicks, whirrs and clicks as the right numbers are found, one by one. Then the tumblers grind and there is one louder click. Matthew reaches out and pushes. The gates swing inward.

The dog bounds through. Meyer gasps, then smiles as he sees it trot up to Matthew and lick his hand.

'OK.' Meyer glances quickly, warily, from side to side. 'Give me a hand, Matthew. The rest of you, get back in the car.'

Matthew and Meyer tug the sleeping bodies of the guards to the grassy verge and toss the guns as far away as they can.

'Which way?' Meyer asks as he climbs back into the car.

'I don't know . . .' Albertine pinches the bridge of her nose between forefinger and thumb. 'Chocky's parent? Are you there? Yes. Hurry. Yes, OK.'

She looks up and points towards a round hillock over to their right. 'That way!'

'Right.'

The back of the seat hits Matthew hard. The children in the back rock forward. The front doors slam shut. The car seems to take a deep breath, then spurts forward, kicking up a wake of grit. The dog gallops alongside.

Already, down on their left where the low huts stand, uniformed men run this way and that. As the car once again comes to a halt, a siren begins to howl. A large door in another artificial hill slides open. There are jeeps and fire engines inside.

'Come on!' Mike is first up the sandy bank to the iron door in the hillside. He pushes at it, then turns to Su Lin. 'Our turn?'

She nods. They too stare at the lock. It too rattles and grinds a bit, then it starts to vibrate, slowly at first, then faster and faster until with a sharp crack the whole lock shatters and falls outward to land at their feet.

Albertine smiles at Matthew. 'The crude approach,' she says.

Then they are in a long corridor of pale breeze-block grey, lit only by bare light bulbs which hang from the ceiling. There are three doors on either side of the passage. Mike tries the first one on the right. A broom cupboard. Meyer tries the first on the left. Some sort of map-room.

'Not those!' Albertine's voice runs on ahead of them up the corridor, 'At the end!'

She points to the large flaking blood red door at the far end of the passage. There is a lot of pattering and shuffling and panting as they run towards it. Their shadows play catch-as-catch-can on the walls.

There is no need for parakinetic lock-picking this time. The door opens readily. Piling through, they find themselves in a sort of high-domed concrete store-room – the central hall of this warren. Plain white wooden crates are piled high in ordered rows. There are perhaps two hundred to choose from, but Albertine points up the right-hand aisle. 'Up there!' she says. The echo of her voice runs fizzing down the walls. The siren outside is very faint in here. She stops again. 'This one?' she asks, then, 'This one.'

With Albertine and Matthew's assistance, Meyer lifts down the crate and lays it gently on the floor. He tugs at one of the wooden sides. It does not give. He looks around for something to use as a crowbar, but Matthew has anticipated his need. He reaches out and touches the wood with one hooked finger, then has to jump quickly back as the whole side of the crate slams to the ground at his feet.

'There it is!' cries Su Lin. 'The pyramid.'

Meyer bends to pull the pyramid out, but even as he does so, he knows that he is too late. There are sharp footsteps outside the door.

'Hold it!' Mrs Gibson's voice slaps at the high vault of the dome. 'None of you is to move an inch.'

Meyer and the children turn. Mrs Gibson wears a smart, severe airforce blue suit and a sour little smile that pushes up one side of her nose. She also holds a smart, severe little black gun which points straight at Meyer's head. She is flanked by two uniformed guards. They too carry guns. Serious guns. Automatic sub-machine guns that could perforate everyone in the room within two seconds.

And incredibly, the guns are being raised. The guards are actually going to shoot. 'You can't!' Meyer stands slowly. His face is white. 'You can't!'

But they can. He knows it. Just as they can leave a child to die alone in a pyramid inside a crate, and they will do it in the name of national security, with the whole complex edifice of national security to cover their tracks and to excuse their conduct.

But a new sound fills the room. The big Alsatian moves forward from Matthew's side. His head is low, his body curved like a bow. His upper lip curls to show yellow teeth. He growls. A deep, vibrant sound that seems to come from his belly.

The guard on the right frowns. For a moment, he lowers his gun. 'Vandal . . . ?' he says. 'Vandal . . . ? Hey, that's Vandal! What's going on here?'

Mrs Gibson makes an impatient clicking sound. The dog draws nearer. His body sinks closer to the ground. Mrs Gibson turns her gun towards him.

The children stand in a row before Meyer. Their faces are quite still.

Suddenly Gibson howls. Her fingers open, the gun flies from her hand and falls to the floor. She clutches her wrist, her mouth stretched wide in a silent scream. The palm of her hand is bright red and shiny. Already blisters bubble up on the stripped flesh.

The guards are yelling too. Molten black plastic covers their hands and drips down their uniforms. The barrels of their guns droop and fall. The man on the left sinks to the floor, keening. His colleague doubles up, whimpers, 'Water . . .' and scurries from the room. His hand steams.

Matthew steps forward. At a silent command, the

dog trots back to his heel. Matthew picks up the revolver, which a moment before had been glowing and smoking. He hands it to Meyer who looks down at it aghast. It is cool.

Outside, the sound of police sirens zig-zags through the constant wail of the alert.

Albertine and Su Lin turn. They wrench away the side of the pyramid. Paul tumbles, very slowly, it seems, into the open air. His face is white. A long brown line of caked blood runs across his forehead. Streaks of blood stain his temple and his nose. Blood has matted his hair.

'Is he all right?' asks Mike.

'He's still alive, anyway,' Su Lin smooths the unconscious boy's hair.

'Chocky,' Albertine calls, 'Chocky, are you there? Are you all right?'

The light that emerges from Paul's head is very dim. It hovers, faintly flickering, just an inch from Su Lin's cheek. *'Yes . . .'* It is a shrill and feeble sound, like an old woman's croak. *'Thank you. We will both be fine.'*

Gibson is sobbing violently by the door. The guard is just staring at what remains of his gun. He gibbers and shakes. His face is stretched in a grimace of terror, his lips rolled back off his teeth. That is how the policemen find them when they run in and relieve Meyer of the gun.

Beatrice Liddle flusters in after them. She throws herself down by her son. Tears drip on to Paul's face from her jawbone. 'Paul,' she sobs, 'oh, Paul, Paul, are you all right? Oh, wake up, please. Say something.'

Paul's eyelashes flutter, then slowly rise. His lips twitch. 'Hello,' he says, then his eyelids prove too heavy and he sinks back into a sleep so deep that it is not disturbed by his mother's hugs and tears and cries.

'She's got to go home for a rest,' Matthew explains to Meyer as they stroll out on to the grass again.

Gibson and the guards have been led whimpering away. An ambulance has borne Paul and his mother to Addenbrooke's Hospital. Mike and Su Lin are already in the police car by the gate. A long ordeal of explanations and half-truths awaits them at the police station.

'But your work?' Meyer asks Albertine.

She shrugs. 'We know enough to be getting on with.'

'So she will be back?'

'Dunno,' she says sadly.

'Yes.' Matthew is pensive. He purses his lips and pauses by the open police car door. He looks up at the combed strands of cirrus cloud that fleck the pale blue sky. 'That's the thing about Chocky. With her, you never know.'